TORTURED HERO

RETRIBUTION GAMES BOOK 5

ELLA MILES

RETRIBUTION GAMES SERIES

Mistaken Hero
Forbidden Princess
Tempted Hero
Fatal Princess
Tortured Hero
Dangerous Princess

1

RI

The words vibrate through my body as I stand in front of a row of men. I want to destroy them all for their roles in my life. For thinking they can control me, just because they're men. For thinking I'm a piece of property, only good for sticking their cocks in and producing male heirs.

But there are also kind men. Men who are just doing their best to lead a group they inherited. Those men simply want to keep their men alive and out of jail.

This group is comprised of men I hate, men I have to kill, and a man I love.

Vincent wants me to show strength. Now that my mind is my own again, I realize why. I remember my purpose, my goal in life. Why I am the way I am—I remember it all.

I also remember why I had to forget for so long and why now is the time to remember. It's a lot to process, a lot to feel, but I know what I have to do.

The gun feels heavier in my hand, heavier than it's ever felt before. I've been trained how to use a gun my entire life for as long as I can remember. Vincent did a lot of the training, but it was nothing compared to what Kek did.

He trained me to not feel emotions, to just do the job. Kill relentlessly to protect, and always protect.

These kills may look like an attack from an outsider's perspective, but they are all about protecting those I love. It doesn't make it any easier for me to pull the trigger, though.

Ryker is my friend. He's protected me even when he didn't have to, but his allegiance is ultimately to his men. He'll throw me under the bus every time if it means protecting his own. But he's a good man, too good of a man—a man who needs to find a way out before an inevitable war starts.

Beckett is the man I love, but he'll never be mine. He's Odette's. Even if he came here to prove he can win me too, it doesn't matter. He's chosen her time and time again, and he'll always choose her over me. But he doesn't deserve to die for loving another woman. I'm not sure I could shoot him even if he did deserve death—I'm too infatuated with him. He'll always feel like my other half, so I need him alive for me to survive what's coming.

The next two men remaining aren't contenders in my head. I skip down the line to my greatest enemy here, and yet the greatest saint.

I turn the gun to him, my eyes welling. He has been kind, way too kind toward me. He's saved me, and I've protected him. He's pushed his limits with me, making it clear he wants me. If I chose him, he'd do everything to make me happy. I thought he was a lovesick, charming man who wanted me while mourning his sister.

I was wrong.

He has betrayed me more than anyone here.

He knew the phrase to fuck with my memories and mind.

I almost died during one of the games because he used the phrase to control me. I couldn't move, couldn't fight back because of him.

He helped Odette escape. He knew from the start she was never dead. He knew exactly where she was and what had happened to her.

He used Odette's death and Beckett's family to start a war.

He pretended to want me when it was so obvious that what he really wants is to kill Vincent and me. The only thing he cares about is putting an end to the Corsi name once and for all.

The Retribution Kings are the enemy. They are the ones wanting to start a war. They're greedy assholes who just want more power.

Caius is my enemy.

But it's harder than it should be to pull the trigger. I've been wrong before, and I could be wrong here. I could be killing an innocent man.

Trust your gut; Kek's words push through me.

I know what my gut is telling me.

Caius is responsible for Lucy's injuries. He's responsible for all of this drama.

I take one deep breath and pull the trigger.

Caius drops, but I don't let my eyes follow him down—part of my training to stay unemotional.

I don't meet anyone else's gaze. I don't want to see the judgment. I don't want to see their fear that I could turn the gun on them next. I could shoot them dead before they could even attempt an attack.

This is what they signed up for when they entered the game, though. Vincent and I are strong. Between the two of us, we could continue the Corsi line. We could control all of these motherfuckers and all of their armies. We are that strong. We are Corsis.

But I'm going to need the strength of all my ancestors to make the next kill. This next one is going to hurt. Not just him, but for me.

He knows it too. He's been begging me to do it for a while. It's his job. It's always been his destiny to protect just like me.

He's not standing in the line against the wall but next to me.

He's a saint.

My saint.

He protected me even when I thought he was trying to kill me. He protected me by training me for the worst situations possible. My nightmares told me he was the enemy, but he was saving me. He was making me stronger, ensuring that when I faced down a dozen men, I would win. He made me strong enough to do the task I was assigned.

And I am because of him.

He's been warning me this entire time, trying to prepare me for the inevitable end. Our destiny was written when I was five years old.

Kek is my saint.

I turn to face him, not sure if I'm doing the right thing. I don't lift my gun right away, and I look Kek in the eyes.

It's a mistake, I know.

Don't get emotional. If you feel threatened, follow your gut. It won't fail.

He's a threat to my goal. He knows too much, a loose end that has outlived his purpose.

But god, why does it have to be me? Why do I have to be the one to kill him?

Why couldn't Vincent do it?

Why couldn't any man here kill him?

I look into Kek's eyes and see him smiling down at me. I know the words he would say if he chose to speak.

This makes you stronger. And these men need to see your absolute strength.

I look at Kek one more time. I remember the darkness of his eyes. I remember the life we had before we had to deal with the real world when we were just training. Before things got messy and complicated, and I needed to forget everything we shared.

I'll never forget you, Kek, never.

He doesn't stop smiling as he gives me the tiniest of nods.

He's ready even if I'm not.

I pull the trigger and turn before the bullet even hits his body. I can't watch. I can't, or I'll no longer show strength. I'll reveal how incredibly weak I actually am. They'll see how much that devastated me, how I'll do anything Vincent wants.

But they can also see how I protect but at the cost of everything.

Everything I love.

Everything I want.

Everything I am.

Anyone in my life who doesn't serve my life's purpose will pay the cost as well.

I walk out the back door of the restaurant's private

room. I hear Vincent's voice boom at the remaining four men behind me.

"If you betray us, you die. If you hurt Rialta's friends, you die. If you start a war, you die—at her hand or mine."

I keep walking. I don't know where I'm going, just far enough away so my show won't be undone a minute later.

I walk out of the building, pausing in an empty alleyway.

Then I fall to my knees and sob.

2

BECKETT

THE ROOM IS silent as Ri walks out of the room. I can't even hear anyone breathing. The reaction is raw, full of shock and heaviness as we all collectively watch Ri strut away.

The mafia princess.

She's supposed to spend her time in fine dresses, attending balls, and bearing heirs. The woman who has mostly hidden her true talents from everyone at her father's orders now shows her true abilities.

She can wield a gun with the best of us.

She can hide her emotions to complete a terrible task.

She can decide for her own who lives and who dies.

She's willing to defy her father when the rest of us cower.

She is strength, and intelligence, and ruthlessness.

She's not just a princess; she's a fighter.

She isn't just owned by the mafia; she is the mafia. We should fear her the same as her father.

That's the message that was sent today. Rialta Corsi is as powerful as any mafia leader, and she's just as vicious.

I don't know why that message needed to be sent so

clearly today when Vincent has been doing his best to make her appear weak so far, but we all got the message.

I stare at the two men dead on the floor. I'm glad Kek is dead, although I'm surprised she killed him. Corsi shockingly didn't step in and scold her for the action. From where I was standing, it appeared Kek was on her side.

Then I turn my gaze toward Caius's body.

My chest swirls with relief but also something else—sorrow. It didn't have to be this way. He helped protect her, but I also suspect he was behind many of her close calls. It wouldn't surprise me if Caius hurt Lucy, if he knew where Odette was the entire time, if he used the phrase to control Ri. He's been pining for her this whole time while also working against her.

But still, I feel sorry for him because I don't think he's the mastermind behind his actions. I think he was just protecting his family, doing what he had to do to be loved by his father and sister.

What a waste.

Ri knew he was a snake, and she killed him. She protected me. She could have just as easily killed me for what she thinks is a betrayal.

She didn't.

She still cares—at least enough to let me live.

She may have done the hard part, but Caius's death is going to be a pain in my ass to deal with.

Corsi steps forward, not the least bit shocked by his daughter's actions. He takes his time, staring each of us down in the eye before he speaks.

"Don't ever try to take my kingdom, my daughter, or my life from me. Ri has been trained for years to defend and kill. She is my right-hand man. I trust her with my life. And if you want to marry my daughter..."

He motions toward the door. "Then you have to accept Ri for who she is. She's not going to let you walk all over her. She's not going to let you control her; she's the fiercest motherfucker here. She will have no problem killing every single one of you, going to the sperm bank, and raising an heir all by herself."

I smirk, knowing he's exactly right. If she needs an heir, she'd rather do it herself than with any of our dumbasses.

"If you want the power of my kingdom, then the game is where you fight for it. There will be no war, no more attacks on people in my family. If you're idiotic enough to ignore these rules, you'll be the next one with a bullet in your head."

Corsi looks at me. "Dispose of your man's body. I have enough to clean up."

I nod.

Corsi starts to walk out the door his daughter just left. "There will only be one more game. I'll be in contact soon." And then he's gone.

Two of the remaining men start cursing and practically run out the door, not able to get out fast enough.

Not me, and not Ryker.

Together we walk over to Caius's body.

"What are you going to do?" Ryker asks me.

"What I've always done—protect Ri."

Ryker nods.

We bend down and lift Caius's lifeless body. She shot him in the heart; he bled out in seconds. His death was quick, which was more than he deserved. Ryker helps me position his body on my back. I'm covered in his blood, so I'll have to explain that I didn't do this.

Dammit, Ri, it would have been easier if you had just killed me.

But then I wouldn't be around to protect her, and I refuse to leave her unprotected.

We start walking toward the door but stop at Kek's body.

"What about him?" Ryker asks.

I frown, still not sure why Ri killed him. I'm missing something because I swear killing Kek was harder for her than killing Caius.

"Leave him. There is nothing we can do for him now."

Ryker helps me load Caius into the back of my car. He doesn't immediately leave. He lingers, something he needs to say on the tip of his tongue.

"Spit it out, Ryker. We don't have all night."

"It has to be you."

"What does?"

"You have to be the winner. You're the one she loves. You're the one she wants. You're—"

"I can't."

"You don't have a choice."

"I'm married to someone else."

"Doesn't matter."

"I have to stay married to protect Ri."

Ryker scoffs like he thinks I'm batshit crazy or something. "Find another way. You two are destined for each other. The only way this ends is with you two together. If you don't, we're all doomed."

Finally, he walks away. He doesn't give me a chance to argue, to say that he's wrong. She should be with him. He hasn't betrayed her, broken her heart, or ruined her for all others. He's a good man. If he loses, he'll end up dead, and he doesn't deserve that.

I'll do everything I can to see Ri happy, and Ryker is her best chance of happiness.

————

I drive back to our hotel. I haven't talked to Gage, Lennox, or Hayes since I returned to Odette's side, but I'm going to need their help now. I send them a group text when I get closer to meet me in the parking lot.

I pull into an empty parking spot at the back of the lot, against some bushes and trees. Only someone standing directly behind my car will be able to see what's in the trunk.

I stand outside, leaning against the side of the car while I wait for the guys. I don't know how any of them are going to react. They've all known Caius a lot longer than I have. They've been friends since they were kids. And yet, they've chosen me over him many times.

But after my recent actions, I'm sure they hate me. Surely, they're going to think I killed Caius.

Finally, I see three shadows approach.

I stiffen as they get closer. All of their faces read undeniable frustration and rage.

My shirt sleeves are rolled up, and my jacket is currently under Caius's body in the trunk, but their eyes roll through me like I'm naked. As if they already know what happened and judge me responsible.

None of us speak. I walk to the back of my car and pop the trunk. I step back, waiting for the attacks, punches, and guns to be pulled on me in vengeance.

Hayes, Gage, and Lennox all walk closer as they stare down at their dead childhood friend.

I open my mouth to say I'm sorry, *but what is that going*

to do? It's not going to bring him back or change any of my actions.

So I'm silent. They are too.

A strong wind brushes through us before Hayes finally breaks the silence.

"Ri?"

"Alive," I respond.

He nods; that's all he cares about. Apparently, that's all any of them care about anymore—Ri. She's the only thing pure between us.

I swallow down the dryness in my throat. "She killed him."

Hayes nods as if he already knew that.

Gage stiffens.

Lennox swears under his breath.

"Well, it's not like he didn't deserve it," Gage finally says.

Everyone chuckles through wet tears.

Their feelings toward Caius were complicated. He was a friend and an enemy; their leader and their villain.

"What do we do now?" I ask as I realize a tear has escaped my eye as well. I wipe it away quickly before the others notice that I mourn Caius's death just like they do.

"We? Are we a 'we' again?" Hayes asks with a grin.

"We were never not a 'we,'" I growl back.

He chuckles. "Sure seems like we haven't been a 'we' since you took Odette back and cut us out of the loop. What the hell?"

I rub the back of my neck, not sure if I should tell them what happened or not.

"Really? Are you still not going to talk to us? Fine, you can figure this out yourself," Hayes grumbles, starting to walk away.

Lennox grabs the back of his shirt and pulls him back. "You aren't going anywhere, and Beckett will tell us what he needs to tell us."

Gage is quiet, but he just stares at me with disappointment in his eyes.

"I did it for Ri, okay?"

"What?" Hayes spits out.

"I'm with Odette to protect Ri. I can't tell you more than that without risking the deal and Ri's life, but that's why I'm with her."

The tears are back.

Damn, fucking tears.

I push through. "I love Ri with everything inside me, but I can never be with her. I'm not good for her, and the circumstances... If I chose Ri, she'd end up dead, and I refuse to let that happen."

Hayes's mouth drops.

Lennox and Gage stare silently, taking in my words.

"I can't tell you more. I can't give you the specifics. If you knew them, you wouldn't want to know because I know you all care about Ri too."

They nod.

"You have to trust me. If you want to protect Ri, then you have to trust me."

"Okay," Gage says first, followed by begrudging agreements from both Hayes and Lennox.

"Thank you."

"What now?" Hayes asks.

"Now, we help Ryker win, and we keep protecting Ri in the process."

"Ryker? Really?" Lennox asks.

I nod. "He's the best guy left in the game, you all know that. He won't pressure her. He just wants to protect his own. She'll have as much freedom as she wants."

All three of them stare back at me like I'm insane.

"Dude, all she wants is you. Anything less won't be enough for her," Hayes says.

I frown. "She loves me, sure, but she's strong enough to find a fulfilling life without me."

"Maybe, but she'll never love again," Lennox chimes in.

"Love is overrated," I say.

We all turn back to Caius's body.

"Now, what do we do about him? Everyone is going to think I killed him."

"So let them," Gage says.

We all turn to him. I cock an eyebrow. "How does that help me stay in control of the Retribution Kings and not get killed?"

"For one, you don't really care about either of those things, but neither of them will happen. And two, your main job is to protect Ri. If you tell anyone that Ri killed him, then you'll start another war for sure. Then you can't guarantee Ri's safety."

He's right.

I need to do everything I can to protect Ri, even if that means telling everyone I killed Caius.

"They won't kill you. You are the leader. You're going to war with your brother in retribution. If you say Caius was attacking you or threatening that goal in any way, they'll have no choice but to believe you. If you said Caius needed to die, then Caius needed to die."

I agree, although sometimes I think an all-out war is exactly what we need. Ri is strong and capable. She could win in a war—even get free, real freedom, if her father and other mafia leaders died.

But it's too risky. I won't risk her life for a chance of freedom.

I do sometimes wonder if it's time the whole world burns. Only the strong and worthy would survive the fires of hell.

"There is only one problem—what do I tell Odette? She's going to want to kill me either way."

"Will she? She needs you. And you have a deal with her to keep Ri alive and safe, so use it."

I nod, but it's easier said than done. I'm the only one who knows the real Odette and just how vengeful she can be.

3

RI

I WALK DOWN the long hallways smudged with tan boring paint. I don't know why anyone would choose this color for a place supposed to be full of hope and healing. Instead, it makes me want to puke and run in the opposite direction.

Maybe that's actually what they're going for here. Instead of giving you hope and peace, they terrify you to convince you to heal faster and get your ass out of their hospital bed.

I'm a mess. I should have changed out of my dress. I should have washed the ruined mascara off my face, or at least first washed off the stench of death before coming. But I couldn't wait. I need to see how she's doing. I need more truths.

One of Vincent's men is stationed outside her room, ensuring her safety as long as she's here. At least she'll be protected from physical threats, although no one can help much with whatever is happening internally.

He nods at me when I walk past him. I don't speak to him as I reach for the door handle.

Does he know what I've done? Was he friends with Kek? Did they train together?

I can't think about that.

What's done is done.

I did what I had to do. I'm no better than anyone else, but at least I serve a purpose. I've always had a goal, and I'll do everything I can to achieve it.

I push the door open and carefully walk inside. I don't want to wake Lucy if she's asleep. But before I take more than a step inside, Loki greets me, full paws up on my chest and almost knocking me back.

"Hey, boy," I say with a smile, glad that Vincent found Loki to keep Lucy company. "How's she doing?"

He wags his tail at me as I enter the room.

Lucy is asleep in the hospital bed. Tubes are connected to her arms and chest, and yet she looks so peaceful.

I could check her chart or ask a nurse what's wrong with her, but that won't help Lucy. Instead, I sit in the chair next to her bed and hold her hand. Loki jumps up on the bed next to Lucy and curls up.

I sigh as I stare at her.

"Oh, Lucy. Why didn't you tell me the truth? Why hide everything from me?"

I already know the answer. It's the same reason I made myself forget.

To protect something greater than both of us, something that we love more than life itself, something pure and worthy.

Protection will cost us everything, but it's worth it.

"You need to hang on, Luce. Just a little longer, and then this is all over. Then you can live your life again."

I swear I hear her moan. It's so soft I'm not sure I actually heard it, but it doesn't seem that she agrees with me.

I frown.

She needs to live. She's the only one left in this world with me.

I don't know why Caius attacked her. I don't know what he was looking for, what information he thought he could get out of her, but I know she didn't tell him. She hid the truth just like I did.

I hear the door open and close. I expect it to be a nurse or doctor, but I know from how silently the person is moving that it's Vincent.

I stare up at him. He probably wants to talk to me, punish me for killing Kek.

I stand without him asking and follow him out of the room. We walk a bit down the hallway until he turns into what appears to be a staff break room but is completely empty. Vincent starts pouring us cups of coffee.

"I'm sorry—" I start.

"Don't be," Vincent responds.

I open my mouth and then slam it shut, flabbergasted. I blink.

Maybe I'm hallucinating?

Every time I blink, he's still standing there looking at me with approving eyes.

Huh.

I take the cup of coffee he offers me, even though I need sleep, not caffeine, to stay awake.

"You did the right thing. Kek was a weak link. He was tortured by keeping our secrets and the darkness he had to become to help you. He hated himself for what he did to you, hated all the pain he inflicted. He would have snapped eventually. You did him a kindness by killing him and ending his misery."

"He didn't deserve to die."

"I know, but he needed to."

Kek needed to die.

I'm not sure anyone needs to die.

"I didn't do it because I was upset with all the things he did. I did it because I saw his pain, and I knew he was tired. He couldn't do the job anymore."

Vincent nods. "As I said, you did the right thing. And the others respect you more for shooting your own man when he went against you."

"Kek never went against me."

"I know that, but the men will assume he did and respect you even more for it."

"So now I get to be who I truly am? Do I get to show off all my skills? Show how strong I am?"

"Yes. Make the men fear you."

I let that thought settle as I sip the cheap coffee.

"You remember everything?" Vincent asks.

"Yes, Kek released me before I killed him. Was he wrong to do that? Should he have waited?"

"No. Now is the time."

I look past him to the door. All I want right now is to go check on Lucy, curl up in the chair next to her, and sleep.

"You still on board with the plan?" Vincent asks.

I frown. How dare he ask me that after everything I've sacrificed. "Yes, I've always been a good soldier."

He smirks. "That you are."

"How are we ending this game?"

"I'm not sure you're going to like my plan."

"I never like any of your plans, but I still follow them."

He gives me a condescending look. "Until you take matters into your own hands."

I shrug. "That's why you like me."

He smiles, and I know it's true.

"There will be one final game. We are running out of time, and I want everything settled—"

A dog's bark in the distance stops him mid-sentence.

"Lucy!" I scream in a panicked voice.

I run into the hallway and down to her room.

I'm not the only one running. Nurses, doctors, and other medical professionals all flood into her room.

I try to run inside, but one of them stops me.

"Loki, come!" I yell into the room, knowing he's not helping.

For once, he listens to me.

"Good boy." I kneel next to him outside the door and rub his neck. We both listen intently to them working on Lucy, unsure if she's going to live or die.

I look over at her guard.

"Did anyone enter?" I ask.

"No, of course not," he says in a frantic voice, afraid I'm going to kill him if I find out otherwise. Apparently, news of what I've done travels fast.

I ignore him. I'm not going to kill him, but Vincent might if he fucked up.

Vincent finally makes his way down the hallway to where I'm crouched against the wall feeling helpless.

"Lucy thought she was safe. She thought no one would harm her, no matter what. That's what she told me. Why did she think that?"

I look up at Vincent.

He looks down at me sternly. I'm not going to get an answer from him, at least not right now.

I hear a loud flat beep; Lucy's heart gave out.

I hear frantic words of doctors and nurses trying one more time to save her.

I hear the exhaustion in their voices, and I know the outcome.

"She didn't want you to worry. I tried to train her as I trained you, but she didn't have your raw talent or strength. Since she couldn't protect herself, all she wanted was to ensure you were happy and could do your job.

"Just like Kek, she was willing to make the ultimate sacrifice. Death meant nothing to her if it meant keeping you safe. You're the only one who needs to stay alive now."

I hear a doctor call out her time of death.

Tears drip down my cheek in a flood.

Lucy gave her life to the cause, just like Kek. Vincent will one day, too, as will I.

We all need to stay alive until we don't.

I'll be the last to die, but I'll die too. Maybe then I'll learn if all of our sacrifices were worth it.

4

BECKETT

"ODETTE?" I whisper into the darkness of our hotel suite.

"You don't have to whisper. I wasn't going to sleep until you got back." Odette walks over to me and kisses me on the lips before I have a chance to react. This is my life now —being kissed and touched by a woman I hate to protect a woman I love.

"I'm glad you made it out safely. Now you can pull out of the game. I'm sure my brother can win without your help. There can't be that many rounds left."

I hold out my hand to her, a gesture I only do in public when I need to play the part. "Come with me."

She frowns. "It's the middle of the night."

"I know." I continue to hold my hand out, insisting she come with me.

I may not like Odette very much right now, and my feelings for Caius were complicated, but I still feel sorry for her. This is going to hurt her. She and her brother were close, and losing him will wreck her.

Reluctantly, she takes my hand, and I silently lead her out of the hotel. She doesn't ask any questions. Somehow, she senses what awaits her. If she's silent for a little longer, then she can avoid the pain for a few more seconds.

I understand. I've been in that situation countless times.

But this time, she needs to face the truth—the faster, the better. The morning will be easier if she deals with the bulk of the pain now, in the darkness.

I lead her to the back of my car and pop the trunk.

For most people, showing them their dead loved one is the wrong move. It's harsh, and the memory they keep is not one they want to remember. But in this case and in our world, we want the truth. We don't shy away from reality, from the pain.

And usually, the only way we truly believe someone is dead is if we see the body—maybe not even then. I look at Odette and think of the picture and the body we buried I thought was hers.

She doesn't fall apart right away. She's stronger than that.

She reaches her hand out and strokes Caius's hair off his forehead. His face looks peaceful, like he's just asleep, not dead. The rest of his body is what carries the marks of reality. The blood and open wound in his chest explain what really happened.

She lets her hand run down his face and then over some of the blood.

I take a step back, giving her space to process however she needs to—cry, scream, anything.

It turns out Odette is stronger than I thought. She doesn't let any emotion out at all. She's as solid as ice. Her heart doesn't break at all, at least not from where I'm standing.

It takes longer for reality to set in for some people,

maybe what's happening here. But I don't think she'll break later either—at least, not in the traditional tears and wailing kind of way.

"How?" she asks, her voice low and deep.

"We were playing the game. He attacked me. I had no choice but to defend myself. I'm so sorry, Odette. He was like a brother to me. I never meant for him to die." The words aren't the complete truth, but they're what she needs to hear—remorse.

She laughs.

Laughs.

She's diabolical.

I grip my gun, ready for anything.

She turns and looks me dead in the eyes. "Don't lie to me."

"I'm not lying."

"For one, Caius and I were blackmailing you into doing what we wanted. Don't feed me that bullshit about him being like a brother to you."

"Fine, but I still cared about him. I didn't want him to die. I don't think Caius was an evil man; I just think he was being pressured to do what you said."

"More lies."

I frown.

"You know what I think?" she asks, stepping closer to me, outrage threatening in her voice. Apparently, her depression from losing her brother is going to come out as anger, not sadness. Unluckily, I'm the one she plans to take her wrath out on.

I don't move. I won't cower in front of her. I won't show fear. She wants a fight; I'll win.

Me, not her.

She's won too many times, way too many fucking times. Just give me a reason to fight, and I'll take it.

"I think your precious whore of a girlfriend killed him."

I cross my arm over my chest, not looking the least bit fazed. I can't let her know she's right. I'll protect Ri at all costs. "She's not a whore, and she's not my girlfriend. Why would she kill Caius? In fact, I'm pretty sure she likes him a lot. She did fuck him after all."

My face wrinkles at that thought. The dead bastard fucked her before I did. She wanted him, even liked him, but she had to kill him. She realized he knew her secret. Odette shared it with him, and neither of them is on our side.

"I don't care who the whore fucked or not. Although, I'm guessing I should get tested because who knows where her cunt has been, and your dick has been inside her."

I glare at her. "Don't call her a whore."

She cackles like a witch. How did I get so fooled by this woman? She couldn't be further away from the angel I thought she was.

"The mafia princess killed him. She found out he knew the truth, and he hurt her friend. She had no choice."

"What do you mean Caius hurt her friend?"

Odette doesn't answer.

"Do you mean Lucy?"

"Is that the blonde bitch's name? Then yes."

"Why did her hurt her?"

She shrugs, looking bored with this part of the conversation. "We needed information from her. But now that he's dead, I have no idea if he got it or not."

I growl. I'm going to kill her.

"I should talk to Stan. We'll figure out a plan to take down the Corsi mafia now that we know for sure they are working against us."

I pull my gun out, no longer playing with her.

Her mouth snaps shut at the sight of the gun.

"You're not going to kill me," she says, staring down the barrel of my gun. Anyone else would say she looks fearless at the moment, but I can see her terror. I can see the way her pupils widen for just a second. She's afraid of dying just like anyone else, and she's not sure what I will do.

"What's stopping me from killing you right now? I got what I needed from you. Ri's safe, and you're the only one left alive who knows how to control her. With you dead, I can get what I really want."

Her mouth curls up in a wicked grin. "You think I'm the only one who knows?" Then there's that damn cackle again that sends vicious tingles down my spine.

"Who did you tell?"

"And why would I tell you that?"

"If you want me to keep you alive, you'll tell me."

"I don't think I will."

"Fine, then I'll kill you."

"That's how you're going to kill me? With your gun? Not very personal. I thought if you did kill me, you'd do it with your bare hands at least. That way, I would feel the heat of your breath on my neck as I take my last breath."

"I wouldn't give you that satisfaction. You mean nothing to me."

She cocks an eyebrow. "Nothing? I thought I was the love of your life? Caius told me about how you wailed when I died, the pain you felt. You mourned me. That is until your whore came along. But before that, you cared. Don't act like you didn't."

"That was before I knew who you really were. You're nothing more than a greedy snake, just like your father and brother."

She laughs. "You don't understand the Retribution Kings at all. We don't want power; we want revenge."

I frown.

"What did my brother ever do to you?"

She licks her bottom lip, but it's a ploy to keep the pain out of her eyes.

I stare at her curiously. He did do something to hurt her. Or at least, she thinks he did.

"What did Corsi do?"

"His sin is more straightforward. He punished my father by taking away a drug shipment that was our main source of revenue. No one trusted us after that. We had to make money the old-fashioned way from that point on—siphoning money from our rich clients. The drugs were so much easier to make money from."

"So what? His daughter deserves to die for that?"

"No, she deserves to die for seducing you into sinking your cock inside of her."

I roll my eyes.

"You don't get to kill her. That's the deal. If you want me to stay your husband and start a war for you, she lives happily ever after, untouched."

"I know, but our deal doesn't extend to her father. You keep playing the game to get close enough to take him out."

"That is if I don't kill you first."

"You won't. If you were going to kill me, you would have already done it. You don't know what precautions I've taken. You don't know who I've instructed to kill her if I die. You can't kill me without killing her."

I frown. I can't tell if she's bluffing or not, but I wouldn't put it past her.

"Tell me the truth—did Enzo hurt you?"

She bats her eyelashes like she's innocent. "He didn't kidnap me. Everything I told you was a lie. But that doesn't mean he doesn't deserve to pay for what he and his family did to me."

"Tell me what they did, and maybe I'll help you willingly."

She shakes her head. "You won't. You're loyal to your family to a fault. It was the same with Caius and me." She looks at his body, and finally, a tear falls. "I never betrayed him, even if he deserved it."

I can't fault her for that, I guess.

"So are you going to kill me and take the chance that Ri will die next? Or are you going to let me clean up your mess, so your sweet princess gets to live a day longer?"

I hate my choices. I want to kill her. But I can't, not until I know if she's speaking the truth. I won't threaten Ri's life.

I lower my gun and then slowly pocket it.

"That's what I thought." She holds out her hand to me like I did to lead her outside.

I brush past her hand, and we walk together back towards the hotel. The whole time we walk, I'm terrified of what Odette is going to demand of me next.

5

———

RI

I'VE BEEN RUNNING for an hour now. I don't know where I'm running; I just let my feet carry me.

Loki is at my side, and he seems just as content to simply run. It keeps our mind off the people we lost.

After Lucy died, I had her guard go get me some running clothes and shoes. Instead of getting the sleep my body needed, I needed to run.

Vincent told me his plan to end the game.

I agreed to it, no matter how difficult it might end up being for me. It is the best way to end the game, so I agreed.

But I'm not thinking about the game as I run.

I'm thinking about Caius.

Kek.

Lucy.

I'm thinking about all the friends I never made.

About all the family I never knew because of who I am and what I chose.

I chose this.

It may not seem like it now as I run through the dark-

31

ness. I have no idea what time it is, but the sun must be coming up soon. It's been dark for too long.

I keep running until I finally realize where I'm running, or more likely who I'm running to.

I stop on the edge of the woods—the same woods I hiked in with Caius before his death.

I should replay his conversation in my head, find out if he was trying to tell me anything before his death. But I can't. It's too painful, even if his death was the easiest of the three I care about.

I slow once we get to the woods. It's dark; only a bit of moonlight lights the path. It's not enough to clearly see where we're going.

I'm panting hard, as is Loki, so we need a break anyway. I don't know where Beckett is. I don't know if he's asleep in the hotel room nearby. I don't know if they went to the cabin or some other secret Retribution Kings head-quarters.

Somehow, he penetrates my thoughts despite every-thing that's happened, despite all the pain.

He confuses me more than anyone.

I thought he loved me.

Then I saw him with Odette and knew I was wrong.

But then he came to the game...*why come to the game?* The prize is me. He already has a wife.

Unless it's to fuck with Vincent somehow? Or help ensure Caius won?

"Are you really there? Or are you a figment of my imagination?" His voice breaks through the thin air. It hits my chest like a sledgehammer, waking me back up from my despair.

"I'm really here. The question is, are you?"

I turn toward the voice, and I can barely see him through the shadows, but he's there.

I step closer.

He does the same.

Finally, we are close enough to make out each other's features.

He's shirtless, wearing running shorts, and is dripping in sweat.

"Seems like we had the same idea," I say.

"It seems that way."

We don't say anything else to each other. *What else is there to say?* I don't trust either of us with the truth.

Loki seems to have a different idea. He pushes forward, giving me no choice but to step closer or yank on the beast's leash.

Loki greets Beckett happily, even though he just lost his best friend. He doesn't let the grief overtake him. He licks Beckett's hand and then jumps up against his chest.

Beckett smiles. "It's good to see you too." He rubs his head and then tells Loki to get down.

He listens and immediately sits at his feet, wagging his tail like he just found his favorite person. He found my favorite person.

And then Beckett looks at me, really looks at me, and he can see everything—straight to my soul.

I think he can see all of my secrets, the truth I've kept hidden my entire life. I think he's going to figure out who I am. He's going to put all the pieces together.

That would be a disaster, but a part of me wants him to. I want to share my secret. I want a life with him, even if it's the one thing I can't have.

He sees me, but he also sees another secret.

"Is Lucy...?" his voice is soft and gentle, begging me to tell him, most likely so he can help me.

But I can't accept his help. If I do, I'll cave. I'll let him manipulate me again. I'll fall for him and give up everything else. But I don't want to lie either.

"She's gone," I say flatly, folding my arms across my chest before he gets any ideas about hugging me.

"I'm sorry. She didn't deserve to die." He takes a deep breath. "None of them did."

"Are you telling me I shouldn't have killed them?"

"No, you did the right thing. I'm saying we all should have lived a much different life. The boys should have been in college, not fighting for their lives."

"And you, what would you do if your life was different?" I can't help but ask.

He takes a deep breath, staring out into the woods. "This," he says when he finally turns back to me. "I'd do this. I'm not a good man, Ri. I lost my arm. I lost my family. This life cost me everything, and yet, I can't imagine doing anything else."

"That's not true; you just don't think you deserve anything else."

The truth bounces back in his eyes. He thinks of himself as a monster, but he's not. I'm still trying to figure out exactly who he is, but he's definitely not a monster.

"I love Odette," he says, seemingly out of nowhere. I know why he said it, though, to get out of the awkwardness of this conversation.

"You do?"

"I do." His eyes pierce mine convincingly. He loves her. He wants her. Even after all the horrors she's done, she's his first love. I'm nothing but a fling to get over her. I should just walk away. I shouldn't stay and listen to anything else he has to say, but I need to hear more. I need to be sure.

"Why did you come to the game then? You have a wife; go live happily ever after with her," my words are harsh and rip through me quickly and sharp.

I take a deep breath while I wait for his answer to calm myself. When I look at Beckett, I expect to see pity in his eyes or the need to hug me. Instead, there's a look of disinterest, like he couldn't care less about my feelings. Maybe he is heartless.

"The Retribution Kings decided we want it all. Even though you didn't hurt Odette, your family has still hurt the Kings in the past. The best way to get revenge is to win the game."

I frown. "If you win the game, then you have to marry me. You can't do that if you're already married."

"No, but I can tell you to marry Gage or Lennox or Hayes. Any one of which would make a good number two in my command."

"They are all back on your side?"

"They were always on my side. They are Retribution Kings until death. Nothing will change that."

I narrow my eyes, not really believing him, but I doubt I'll get a more honest answer from him.

"Why are you acting like a monster?"

"I am one. I'm going to war with my own brother. I'm taking over the Corsi mafia empire. I'm going to rule this world."

Loki tucks his tail and ears back as he makes his way back to my side, not recognizing this new version of Beckett either.

I'm usually a good judge of character. I can usually tell when someone is telling the truth or not. I don't think this is the real Beckett at all, but there is some reason he's pretending it is. I just can't figure out why he's acting this way.

"So you're going to keep playing the game just so you can win and force me to marry one of your friends? Did I get that right?" my voice is bitter and angry.

"Yes."

"What makes you think me or Vincent will go for it?"

"Vincent will agree when there are no other men left. He'll see how powerful I am and won't want to start a war. He said as much at the last game. He'll accept my offer."

"I won't."

He laughs. "You won't have a choice, Princess. Besides, I don't believe you. You've already fucked all of them. From where I was standing, you seemed to enjoy it. So don't tell me you wouldn't want it."

I glare at him. I hate this version of him. *What are you hiding?*

"Good luck with your plan, but it won't work. You can't control three different empires at once."

"Watch me," he growls.

"You won't win. I know what the final game is, and there is no way you can do it."

"I'm stronger than any of the men left, smarter, and more determined. I'll win."

His nostrils flare, and I swear I see a bit of fear. He needs to win. *Why? Why is he so desperate to win?*

I'm done with this conversation, but there is one part left that I need to discuss with him. I'm not sure how he's going to react, though. He may try and kill me right here, right now.

"I need to speak to your wife when she has a moment."

"And why the hell do you need to talk to her? She hates you."

The feeling is mutual, but I don't say that out loud. It won't help anything.

"She has the phrase that can control my mind. I need to ensure she will never use it." She's the only one left who knows it unless she has gone around telling others. But that's a secret too juicy for her to share. She would want the power all to herself."

Beckett grits his teeth, and I can tell he doesn't want to talk about Odette. He doesn't want to drag her into this. He loves her. He truly loves her.

Fuck.

So many fucks.

I should kill Odette. She knows the secret, or if not, she can figure it out.

But I can't, not if he truly loves her.

"Odette won't say anything. She won't do anything. You have my word. She won't use the phrase. She wants nothing to do with you. She won't hurt you in any way."

His words are calm and sincere, but it's not enough.

"Tell me again why you love her. Why you'll do anything in the world for her?"

"Why?"

"Convince me that you love her more than anything else in this world."

"Why?"

"Beckett, just trust me and tell me."

He brushes his hair back in frustration. Apparently, it's torture to share the depths of his heart with me. He opens his mouth and closes it several times before he finally decides where to begin.

"I love Odette because she's the first thing I think

about when I wake up. She's my light, my reason for living." He smiles as he thinks about her, spilling his guts.

"She has this beauty—this incredible beauty. It starts with her outward appearance. From her hair to her curves, to her skin—everything about her is radiant. But it doesn't stop with her appearance; it runs deep, all the way to her heart. She cares deeply about those she loves. She cares about those she shouldn't. She connects with me on a soul level that I can't explain. It's like I've known her my entire life. It's like she was hand-selected for me and me her. She has this fierceness and determination that matches me."

He chuckles, thinking about it. "No, it outdoes mine. She is the strength. She's the boss, the one in control. Though don't tell her that. It will go to her head, and then I'll never hear the end of it."

I smile and nod.

He smiles brighter, thinking about her.

"I love her because she saved me. Time and time again, when I was in my darkest places, she found me there. She made me believe that life was worth living. She kept me from falling over the edge. She's the only reason I would give up this life. I'd give up the Retribution Kings, the game, the war, everything for her. All she'd have to do is ask, and I wouldn't question why; I'd just do it.

"She wants a mansion; it's hers. She wants a tiny house in the middle of the Swedish Fjords; it's hers. She wants a dozen kids; I'll have them with her. She wants none; then she's more than enough for me. Whatever she wants, whatever she needs, I'd give her everything I have. I'd die a million deaths for her to live."

He looks at me darkly, "Don't you dare threaten her life because I don't care who I have to kill to protect her. I'll do anything to protect her, anything to save her. She won't spill your secret. I'll make sure of it. But if you value your life, you won't go near Odette."

His words flood me with the strength of his emotion, of his love for one woman. That's what I've been looking for my entire adult life but never found.

I'm in awe, suddenly feeling tears stinging my eyes. I'm happy for him, really I am.

I grab Loki's leash, and I turn around, ready to jog back home. I got what I subconsciously came here for. On a night where I was left utterly alone by everyone I cared about, I needed to hear this. It solidifies my purpose. It reminds me of what I was born on this earth to do.

"Ri!" Beckett yells.

I turn and look at him, finding fear and complete desperation in his eyes.

"I won't kill Odette," I assure him.

His eyebrow shoots up. "You won't?"

"No, she'll stay alive as long as you love her. But I still need to talk to her," I say against my better judgment.

Then I disappear into the night before I realize my mistake and take it all back. Odette should die, but I won't kill her. I fell in love with a man who will never love me. My happily ever after is different than everyone else's. I don't get to be with the man I love, but I can protect the woman he loves. That will have to be enough to sustain me.

6

BECKETT

I WANTED to pick her up and drag her away and tell her all my truths. I wanted to kiss her, fuck her, make her mine, let her know she's the only woman for me. But I couldn't do any of those things.

I could love her forever if the world were different. Instead, I'm going to be tortured the rest of my life living with a woman I hate. She has the power to destroy the love of my life, and she'll hold that over my head forever.

No, I can't spend the rest of my life tied to Odette. I'll find a way to get free. I'll find a way to make Ri safe once and for all. By then, Ri will be married, though, so Ri will never be mine. But I can still save us both from a lifetime of misery.

As I watch Ri walk away, I realize I'm kidding myself. A lifetime without Ri is a lifetime of misery for me, with or without Odette. Maybe I can be the cool uncle to her kids, still in her life even when she's married. I'm good at playing the uncle role.

God, even that would be torture. Everything about my life will be torture, but it would be better to have her in my life than out.

Slowly walking back to the hotel, I consider returning to my shared room with Odette, but I can't. I can't deal with her touching my body again. Instead, I end up at the room next door.

My knuckles knock against the door, and I'm unsure if anyone is awake. If no one answers, I'll sleep in my car. The guys were dealing with Caius's body, but I suspect they passed out after that.

The door opens to reveal Lennox looking at me. He's fully dressed, not like a man who was just sleeping. He holds the door open for me, and I step inside. I walk straight to the living room couch and flop down on it.

Hayes, Gage, and Lennox all look at me from various spots in the living room.

Hayes looks to the door. "Why aren't you with Odette? Is she sleeping here?" He wrinkles his face in disgust.

Gage hits him in the back of the head.

"Ow!" He rubs the back of his head. "What was that for?"

Gage rolls his eyes. "You know why he's not with Odette. Don't be stupid."

Hayes looks confused as he looks from Gage to me, finally letting out a quiet sigh of understanding.

"The look on your face just now when you thought Odette might be coming here is the same look I have every time she touches me and demands for me to fuck her," I snap.

My heart thumps hard in my chest as silence stretches. I can't believe I just told them that. Slowly, I look to the three guys that have become brothers to me just as much as my own brother.

"Damn, Beckett. We're going to figure a way out of this

mess. And from now on, we're running interference. We aren't letting that witch touch you again," Hayes says.

Gage's eyes darken with a murderous glare.

Lennox looks away uncomfortably. Maybe he has a secret or two of his own to share, but now isn't the time.

"Thank you, but it's my burden to bear. You don't need to worry about it. I shouldn't have said anything," I say.

"Why do you let her touch you at all? I would—" Hayes starts before Lennox gives him an angry look.

"Really? Do you not think before you open your mouth? He has to sleep with Odette to protect Ri. Odette could have Ri killed if Beckett so much as gets into a lover's spat," Lennox answers.

I sit up. "It's okay, really. Anyone got any liquor?"

"Coming right up." Lennox goes to the kitchen and pours a glass of an amber liquid before handing it to me.

"Thanks." I take a sip. I don't want to spend my life drunk, but tonight I need enough liquor to pass out and not run after Ri.

"What happened?" Lennox asks, noticing my mood isn't just about Odette.

"I ran into Ri, and I had to lie to her. I told her I love Odette. I said she can't kill Odette because I love her. When in reality, killing Odette would only kick off whatever contingency plan she has in place to kill Ri." I drink the rest of the glass, letting it burn down my throat, but it's not enough to make me feel. "I played the part, and Ri believed me."

I think about our conversation, about Ri asking me why I love Odette. I couldn't come up with anything, so I told her all the reasons why I love Ri instead. Each word was a dagger to her heart when my words should have been music to her heart. But she got to hear my words, even if she'll never know that they were for her.

Lennox brings the bottle over and pours me another glass, then takes a sip straight from the bottle himself. Hayes grabs the bottle and takes a long sip, passing it to Gage next, who does the same.

"Don't give up hope yet. We all love her—" Hayes starts and then sees the grimace on my face. "I don't mean like that. Yes, we've all fucked her, but that's not what I meant about 'love her.' We know how special she is. And we all know that as much as any of us would be lucky to have her, she's yours. We'll do whatever it takes to make that happen."

"I'm going to need another drink before I tell you my plan." I hold out my hand, and Gage passes me the bottle.

I take a long sip until my head gets a little dizzy. "As much as I want that to be true, I don't know if we have the time to figure out how to take Odette down before Ri gets married. She said there is only one final game."

"Shit. Well, we'll have to work fast," Hayes says.

Lennox stares through me, already knowing what I'm about to say. His jaw tightens. Gage looks to Lennox, the one who can read people the best. Even Hayes eventually looks to Lennox.

"I'm going to keep playing the game. Even Odette wants me to. She wants the Retribution Kings to control everything, starting with the Black Empire and the Corsi Crime Family."

"But you can't marry Ri if you win; you're already married to Odette," Hayes says.

I nod slowly.

"I told her if I win, I'll choose her husband for her," I say.

"Will Corsi go for that?" Gage asks.

"He won't have a choice. I'll make sure there will be no one left in the game for him to choose instead. And I'll threaten war with him if not."

"So, who would you choose?" Hayes asks.

I look from Hayes to Lennox, to Gage. "I'd choose one of you three to marry her."

———

No one really talked after I announced my plan to win and pick one of them to marry Ri. I don't know how I'll choose. I'd let Ri choose, but I don't think she would pick any of them. And right now, it's not my problem. I have to worry about winning first; then I can figure out how to choose.

I have to win—to save her from the other monsters left in the game. Any one of my men would treat her right. Any one of them would let her live her life and have as much freedom as she wanted. Any one of them would do a good job of helping her lead the Corsi mafia. Any one of them could fall in love with her and help her grow to love him in return. Any one of them could make her happy.

Any of them except me.

We walk into the banquet hall where the Retribution Kings are gathered. Odette is talking to one of her friends and scurries over to my side as soon as she sees me. I barely acknowledge her. Hayes, Gage, and Lennox flank me as we walk to the center of the room.

We have to tell everyone what happened last night. We have to lie about why Caius is dead.

I give Odette enough time of day to notice she's decked out in all black and is already letting tears fall for her brother. I'm sure some of the tears are real, but others are part of her performance.

Thankfully, as the fearless leader, I won't be expected to show emotion. I need to appear strong and unbreakable.

"There is an unfortunate reason for our gathering today," I say loudly, drawing everyone's attention. I never thought I'd be able to command an entire room with just my voice, no microphone to make it louder. I never thought I'd be strong enough to endure the stares, but for the first time, I feel like maybe this is what I was born to do. If it wasn't for all the other shit, then maybe I could even enjoy it.

Odette snuggles her way into my chest, and I play the good husband by holding her against me.

"I have to announce that my dear brother-in-law, Caius Monroe, has died."

Murmurs and shock work through the crowd.

"How?" someone shouts at the same time as someone else cries out for retribution.

Odette sobs loudly into my chest, and that seems to quiet them.

"There will be no need for retribution," I say sternly, once again capturing the crowd's attention.

"I killed Caius during Corsi's game. I killed him. I did everything I could, but I didn't have a choice. I regret it bitterly. Caius was like a brother to me. He helped me grieve when I thought I had lost my wife. He helped me become a better leader. He was a good friend."

I see tears in many of the men's and women's eyes as I speak.

"I will finish the game in his honor. I will win to gain us control over Corsi's empire, and I will select one of my closest men to marry Rialta. I will not let Caius die in vain."

Many nod and murmur their agreement. For once, I feel like I'm their leader, and they agree with me.

"Caius is going to be buried in the plot next to his father. I invite you all to follow us to the gravesite. Then return here for food and mourning."

The guys brought Caius's body to the morgue last night to be prepared for burial today.

Odette doesn't say anything, just sobs into me. But it's enough to sell the lie. If she's not arguing with me or saying anything differently, then they believe my story. I killed Caius. I didn't have a choice. I'm devastated that he's gone.

They will never know the truth—Ri killed him. He was a bastard who tried to manipulate her. They will think of him as a loyal Retribution King who would do anything for the cause.

We travel to the gravesite in a caravan. It's strange coming back here. The last time I was here, I thought I was burying Odette. This time, I know for sure I'm burying Caius.

We walk to the site, keeping things simple and not doing a traditional funeral. There wasn't time to do much planning, and this seems right anyway.

Odette's gravestone has been removed, but I still look at the spot on the other side of her father, and my blood boils all over again. I have to let go of Odette for a second when I see her now unused gravesite.

Odette seems to understand and gives me my space.

The ground has already been dug for Caius on the other side of their father. His casket rests suspended above the hole.

Lennox, Hayes, and Gage each say words about losing Caius. They are all truthful, even though they knew what a snake he was in the end. He was still their friend first.

Odette speaks through sobs.

I say a few more words before we lower Caius's body into the ground. We each sprinkle a handful of dirt over his lowered casket.

It's then that I find my eyes have watered.

I look at Odette standing in front of Caius's lowered casket. His death is because of her. She orchestrated everything. She is the one who wanted power, control.

I vow right now that she will be back where she belongs—in the ground next to her father.

7

RI

VINCENT GAVE us a couple of days off before the next game. I think after the last one, we all needed it.

Time to mourn.

Time to collect our thoughts.

Time to regroup and strategize.

Just time to live.

I stand in front of Lucy's headstone while Loki lays in the grass in front of it. My time to mourn is up; I have a job to do. But in a way, I'll never stop mourning what I've lost.

"I'll never forget you," I say, putting my hand on the stone. "Caius initially hurt you, but the doctor said you were fine before you crashed. I'll make sure whoever killed you pays."

Loki moans.

"And I'll take care of Loki for you, don't you worry." I scratch his head, and then we start heading back to the car.

I pass Kek's grave as I walk back to the car, but I don't stop. His death is so much more painful because I had a choice. I could have let him live—I didn't. I'm not ready to face that reality yet.

I open the car's driver-side door for myself but find Loki jumping in first. He climbs over to the passenger seat, even though he has a lot more room in the back seat. I roll his window down after he paws at the window, and then we're off.

I don't have any guards. Vincent is no longer pretending that I need them. He knows I'm more capable than any guard he has.

And despite not wanting to play the last game, Vincent knows I'll show up. I won't run. I won't shirk my responsibilities. As much as I'm tired of playing games, I'm ready for this to all be over.

It will never be over, though. This is my life, and it will never stop.

At least there won't be any more games.

Today is the final game. I drive to the same restaurant where the last games were held, where I shot three people dead. I didn't want the next game to happen here too, but Vincent said it would remind the men of what happened last time and how strong I am.

I didn't argue, although I don't know how they could forget me killing in front of them. All it's going to do is mess with my head.

I park in the parking lot and look at Loki.

"Ready?"

He wags his tail in response.

I open my door, and he jumps out after me, landing awkwardly as he does. It makes me smile.

"Come on," I say, not bothering to put a leash on him. He hasn't strayed from my side since Lucy died. I'm guessing he has separation anxiety, but I haven't had time to bring him to a vet to see how to help him.

We walk side by side into the restaurant just as the clock strikes seven. I didn't want to show up a second early or a second late.

I hold my head high, walking into the room where the remaining four men stand.

The room is silent; all eyes are on me as I enter. Thankfully I haven't cried today, so my eyes aren't puffy. There is no sign of the mourning I've been going through this week, nor are there any other signs of weakness.

Loki stares down all the men, baring his teeth at some of them as I walk to Vincent's side. Loki growls at one of the men, and he flinches.

I smile and pat Loki's head. "Good boy."

We stop next to Vincent.

"You ready?" he asks me.

"I was born ready."

He gives me a knowing smile. "I know; that's why I picked you."

I turn solemnly to the crowd of men who are spread out in front of us. They're all dressed up again in suits and tuxes. *Maybe they think they're making less work for the mortician after I kill them?*

I spot Ryker, who is, as usual, playing his part of acting like he couldn't care less, and he's above this all.

Next to him is a guy I wouldn't let near me—Hogan. Cruel and ruthless, he has no redeeming qualities. His men are loyal to him strictly out of fear, not loyalty. He has no chance of winning this game or my heart.

And then there is Beckett. He winks at me when I look at him. *Does he think he's somehow doing me a favor by being here?* He has no idea that he can't win. Vincent would never allow him to choose one of his friends for me to marry instead of him. If he wins, Vincent will make his marriage to Odette disappear. That's not what Beckett wants, so I won't let it happen.

The final man, standing off to the side, is one I barely know. He doesn't look intimidating, but he's not cowering in terror, afraid I'm about to shoot him. He's the only one whose name escapes me. Maybe I need to take a closer look at him.

"Thank you all for keeping to the rules this week. I'm glad to report no scheming or wars have been started this week, so there's no need for Rialta to kill anyone to start off the game."

I give the room a seductive, disappointed smile that says I'd love to shoot and kill again.

Hogan swallows hard, sweat beading off his forehead.

I smirk; he's a dead man.

"We have decided there will be one final game. Rialta's birthday is coming up soon, and she's anxious to get married," Vincent continues.

Ryker and no name both grin cockily, thinking they will be the one I marry. They're probably right. Either of them is the current front runners in my book.

Unfortunately, I don't know what the exact rules of this game even are. I get the general idea, but I don't know if Vincent or I will be declaring the winner.

"The game is simple. In fact, it's the easiest game we've played so far. Scoring is very objective, and soon we will have a clear winner," Vincent says, drawing out the men's anxiety.

"Although the game is simple, it's not any less dangerous. There are no rules. Hurt, betray or kill anyone in this room. Do whatever you have to do to win. If you lose, you'll probably end up dead."

The men start eyeing each other with deadly unsaid threats. I roll my eyes.

"As I've said before, the winner gets to marry my daughter, Rialta Corsi, and take control of my empire as soon as they produce a male heir to continue my legacy." Vincent looks to me, silently waiting for me to back out.

I know how risky this game is; I know what's at stake. But we have to know who the right guy is, and this is the best way to figure it out.

If I had to choose right now, I'd pick Ryker. *But do I really know him? Could he have tricked me all along? Could I have been blinded by his good looks and my need to get back at Beckett?*

Could the mystery man be better?

And then my gaze turns to Beckett. He would have been perfect. One tiny thing got in the way, unfortunately —he loves another woman.

Choosing the man to win isn't about love. It should be about finding the best man for the job. The man that will make the best husband. The man who will fight to the death to protect his family. The man who will do the best job in following in Vincent's footsteps. The man who will become a leader feared by the outside world but also supported by unending respect earned from his own men.

If I listen to my heart, Beckett is that man. But that's why I'm not listening to my heart anymore. I'm listening to my head.

Ryker.

It has to be Ryker.

I should talk to Vincent about my thoughts, see if he agrees.

"There are two ways to win the final game," Vincent speaks again.

I lock eyes with Beckett, wanting to see his reaction more than anything. I know Ryker won't break face when Vincent announces the game. I should look at the mystery man to see his reaction, but I don't know him well enough to know if he can fake his emotions or not. But Beckett—he can't hide from me. He can't hide his reactions, not fully.

"The first way to win is the most straightforward."

Here it is—the moment I've been dreading.

I suck in a deep breath so I can keep my own reaction flat.

"To win, you have to be the one to get her pregnant," Vincent says, motioning to me.

I don't see anyone's reaction but Beckett's. His is the only one that matters. His eyes dilate. His nostrils flare. His hand fists so hard that I think he's going to break his own bones.

He's pissed.

If he doesn't get control over it, he'll start fighting every man in this room to the death right here.

It's the action of a man who cares—*a man who might even love?*

Curious.

Quickly, he regains control of his emotions. The rage and fury are still there under the surface, but anyone else looking at him would think he doesn't care. His eyes are now scanning my body, thinking about strategy. His eyes land on my arm, where I told him I had birth control implanted. The same place where he shot me.

His eyes examine my body, maybe trying to figure out if he already got me pregnant. *Does he think he's already won?* Or maybe he's considering how low his chances of winning might be since he's fucked me numerous times without protection and didn't get me pregnant.

Beckett says he loves Odette, and after that impassioned speech, I believe him. But this will be the ultimate test of that love. If he loves her, he won't touch me, even to win. And if he doesn't...

"Any questions?" Vincent asks the room.

"So, we're supposed to kidnap her and then rape her until we get her pregnant?" Hogan asks.

Vincent shrugs. "That's one option."

I feel everyone's eyes on me, reading my reaction. I'm stone-cold; I won't be getting raped. At least, I'll do everything I can to not be. And I'd bet on my skills against any man here.

They can try, but I'll cut off their dicks for daring to touch me without my permission.

"How do we prove we're the one that got her pregnant?" Hogan asks.

"Don't worry about that. We'll know. And if it isn't obvious, there are always tests that can be done," Vincent answers.

I stare down the men, just teasing them to try and fuck me without my permission. Loki is doing the same thing next to me, almost like he understands the words Vincent spoke and won't be letting any man near me.

Ryker steps forward. "You said there are two ways for us to win. What is the other objective?"

Vincent looks at me out of the corner of his eye, and I can read what he isn't saying. I know the other way to win instinctually. If it's up to me, this will be the way the victor will win.

"The second way you can win will remain a mystery. It's something you will have to figure out for yourself."

"That's not fair; how are we supposed to win if we don't know all the rules?" Hogan asks.

"This game was never designed to be fair. It was designed to find the best man for the job. You want to win? Then figure it out."

Vincent quickly exits the room, leaving Loki and me standing in front of the men alone.

I can see Beckett's eyes again, this time asking a million questions. *The most important one is why? Why would I agree to a game where I could end up raped?*

I don't answer him. I don't give him any more clues than the other guys.

The guys expect me to run, to shriek in terror that they may gang up on me and all take turns raping me right now just to get the game over with. But I'm done running. I'll never run again.

"Good luck, boys," I say. Then I turn and casually walk out the door after Vincent with Loki by my side. The men are left speechless with their mouths agape, not having a clue what to do next. But they'll figure it out soon, and then the game will really start.

BECKETT

WHAT. The. Hell.

What the hell is happening?

Impregnate her? That's how we win? That's INSANE.

It's even more insane when you consider how calm Ri was about it. She knew it was coming. It was clear that she and Corsi had talked about it beforehand. She should have argued with Vincent after his announcement and tried to stop it from happening.

She didn't.

She accepted it as easily as she did any of the other games.

I'm missing something.

I must have misheard the rules.

Yes, that's it.

Except, I didn't.

I heard correctly.

The game is simple—get Ri pregnant by any means.

Fuck!

Now, what the hell do I do?

I can't let Ri know I still love her, that it's always been her. I have to convince her I'm in love with Odette. It's the only way to protect her until I figure out how to take down Odette without harming Ri.

Does Ri already know? Or at least suspect?

The way she looked at me just now made it look like she thought I was full of shit. But before she seemed so convinced—I don't know.

Still, I can't get Ri pregnant while married to Odette. Odette would kill her if she found out what I did, even to win the game. And it's not like Ri would let me touch her anyway.

Unless...

Ri hasn't been on birth control since I shot her in the arm. I could read the truth in her eyes when I stared at the scar on her bicep.

Is she already pregnant?

That's even more of a nightmare. I don't want kids. I've seen my brother and his friends try to raise kids while being involved in organized crime, and it never works out. They are never safe.

I love being an uncle. I love watching the kids and taking care of them, but I'm not sure I'm cut out to be a dad.

But if Ri was carrying my kid...fuck, I would do anything for that kid.

Anything.

I just don't know what the truth is.

We all stand in shocked silence, silently watching Ri walk out of the room like she's not about to have six men and everyone who works for them come to rape her.

My stomach curls at the thought.

Fuck.

Suddenly, I feel everything coming up. The acid in my stomach hits me first and then the pasta that Hayes cooked for dinner.

I push it all down, ignoring how I want to do nothing but vomit. I have to figure out a plan before these bastards do.

Smack.

I feel my jaw come unhinged as pressure builds in my face, and I fall back. The only thing keeping me from falling on my ass is the wall I slam into behind me.

Another punch connects with my eye socket before I can react. If I wasn't in such a state of shock about what just happened, then maybe I would have been better prepared for this outcome—but I wasn't.

I throw my own arm up, blocking another punch before I kick the asshole's legs out from under him. He falls hard, but I don't let up, continuing to kick him as I realize an all-out brawl has broken out. Weapons are being drawn—it's a fight to see who is going to get their hands on Ri first.

I pull out my own gun and duck as a bullet whizzes past me. I squat, trying to use Hogan's moaning body on the ground as my shield while I fire back.

The last remaining man is firing right at me. It seems he thinks I'm his biggest threat.

I can take him down, though.

A dozen men start filing into the room, and now I'm not so confident. My team is nearby, but I won't call them into a situation where they are vastly outnumbered and have a high probability of dying. I'm on my own.

"Beckett!" I hear someone shout.

I flick my head in his direction but keep firing to keep from being shot to death.

Ryker.

He has three men around him firing.

"Let's go!" he shouts. I realize he's waiting to help me escape. Ryker deserves to win, not me, not anyone else—him. I just need to figure out if that's what Ri wants—Ryker. Or if she'd rather have Lennox, Hayes, or Gage. I'll give her any man in the world she wants; it just won't be me.

I stay low to the ground as I run as fast as I can toward Ryker and his men. They cover me, and then I'm out the door just as his men slam it shut.

We sprint out of the back of the restaurant and into the alleyway. That's when my team finds us.

"What the hell happened to you? I thought you could fight better than that," Hayes says.

"I can," I growl.

Hayes motions to Gage, who is wearing a backpack full of gear. The next thing I know, Hayes has an ice pack out and is pressing it against my face.

"I'm fine," I say, pushing his hand away.

"You won't be able to see tomorrow if you don't get the swelling down. And you might need your sight, so you don't lose another fight."

I roll my eyes but press the ice pack against my face.

"Thanks, Ryker. You didn't have to save my ass back there," I say.

"I did because I don't know what the hell to do next. I need an ally."

I nod. "Then you have one."

"Good, now what?" Ryker asks.

I chuckle. "I have no fucking idea. We have to be missing something, right?"

"I would think so, but nothing about this whole game makes any sense."

"What happened? Is the game over already? Who won?" Hayes asks.

We ignore him.

"You going to fuck her?" Ryker asks.

I smirk. "She wouldn't allow it. You?"

"Not unless she begs me to, but that won't stop the others. I know she's tough. I've seen it first hand. She's stronger than any chick I've ever met, but this is different. This is the final game. This is between winning everything—her, the empire, ultimate power—and most likely death. Everyone who has lost is now dead. This round won't be any different."

He's right, but I don't say that. Ri can take on a lot of men, but if all of a gang is after her, she doesn't stand a chance. She can't fight and take down an entire organized crime family as much as she thinks she can. She does have weaknesses, and eventually, one of the men will catch her. Once they do, she's screwed.

She needs a hero.

I'm no hero.

I've told her time and time again; I'm not hers.

But maybe it's time to play the hero. Maybe it's time to knock some sense into her. I'll give her a choice—Ryker, Lennox, Hayes, or Gage. Any one of them will do, but she has to pick. She has to tell us how to win without impregnating her. Because I can't fuck her while married to Odette if she wants Lennox, Hayes, or Gage. And if she wants Ryker, it could take months for him to get her pregnant. It's too risky to let the game go on that long.

We need to find the fastest way to end this game.

"We go after her and catch her before the others," I say.

"You mean kidnap her against her will?"

I nod.

Ryker laughs. "I'm going to enjoy watching her castrate you."

9

———

RI

A BATTLE BREAKS out behind me. I hear guns going off and the scuffle of hands and fists hitting each other. Maybe they'll all kill each other, and I can forget this stupid game.

No, we need a winner.

Had Nico not died, we wouldn't have had to do these games. *Was he perfect?* No, but he would have done the job well. He was loyal and trustworthy. He was vicious when he needed to be, but not too power-hungry. He wasn't horrible to look at either, but there were no butterflies, no passion. It would have been only a job arrangement.

That's how I need to think of this—find the best business partner.

I cringe as I hear more bullets flying behind me. The best business partner needs to be able to survive a little fight. I can't think about who might be hurt, injured, or dying in there right now.

"They're all still boys. None of them are acting like men," Vincent says.

I nod and pet Loki's head next to me to keep from thinking about the guys. I want to ask Vincent the exact

63

rules. I want to know how much power I have in deciding my fate, but I'm too scared to ask.

Vincent looks me in the eyes, and I know...I have all the control I could possibly want. Just get through this final game, and I'll have my life back. Or at least, my role will be more settled.

The battle gets louder behind me. I don't want to be here when someone emerges from the door. I have to make it a little harder for them than that.

I look down at Loki. I won't let him get hurt in the process.

"Stay," I tell him and then look purposefully at Vincent.

He sighs and rolls his eyes, but he'll take good care of Loki.

I smile and then jog off.

———

Apparently, I made it too hard for any of them to find me because it's been three days, and I'm bored to tears. I've been renting an extravagant, fully furnished condo for the last three days, ordering room service, going to the spa every day, and soaking in the oversized tub every night.

But I'm getting tired of not having a purpose during my day. I'm getting tired of waiting to find out which guy will find me first. I'm getting tired of chocolates, wine, and watching Netflix.

Lying on the bed, I'm staring up at the light fixture in the bedroom. It's a chandelier with hundreds of little lights. It's nighttime, and I've turned the light off, but I can see the reflection of the moon through the window hitting each light individually. *Why does a fixture need so many lights? What's the purpose? To just look pretty and produce heirs?*

Some women want this—a life of luxury and pampering where their only job is to look pretty and get pregnant as soon as possible.

I scrunch my nose at that, not me.

Giving up on sleep, I get up and walk outside to the balcony overlooking the river below. I rest my forearms on the railing. I've never been afraid of heights, but there is something about being so high up when you're at a crossroads in your life. It would be so easy to end it on my own terms, to not let anyone control me ever again.

A shadow moves behind me—finally.

I glance down at my arms. No hairs are raised. I don't have goosebumps, no chills race down my spine. I know who it's not—only one man gives my body that reaction.

So who is it?

I turn just as his hand grabs onto my neck, and I grab onto his.

"Mystery man," I say.

He raises a cocky eyebrow. "You don't remember me, sweetheart?"

I shrug. "There have been a lot of guys. Sorry, you weren't that memorable."

"Then I did my job well. My goal was to make it to the finals without being noticed. Only now will I fight to win."

"Do I get your name?"

"Sure, but only so I can have the pleasure of hearing you yell it out over and over again when I fuck you. It's Elias Roberts."

My features turn dark. "I won't be calling out your name, and you won't be fucking me."

"I think I will. I want to win. I don't want to die. If I

lose, I die. So I won't lose. And you'll be calling out my name, alright. Either out of pleasure or pain—I'll take either." His lips curl until I see the whites of teeth. His front teeth are crooked, just like him.

"Then you should have brought more men to capture me, Elias." I break his hold before kicking him hard in the stomach. I enjoy the sight of watching him double over in pain.

I was hoping that Elias was some saint, the perfect man for the job. It would make things less complicated, but he's not. He's a monster, just like the rest of them.

Actually, he's scared shitless and will do anything to protect his own skin—the exact opposite of what you want in a leader.

I run inside and stop in my tracks. My apartment is flooded with armed men. I can't even count all of them. There has to be at least twenty, no thirty, plus men—all with their guns pointed at me.

I roll my eyes. Well, this is way more than what was needed.

I turn around just as Elias walks inside.

"I brought plenty of backup," he says with a sly smirk.

I slow clap like I'm impressed. "Good job. You did one thing right. It doesn't mean you're going to fuck me. And it doesn't mean you're going to win."

"Actually, it does," Elias says as I feel hands descend on me.

———

I wake up freezing cold. My entire body is trembling so violently that my teeth are chattering. My head is fuzzy;

they must have drugged me. But I'm not sure that's the source of my shivering body.

I force my eyes open to face the reality of my situation. It's as perilous as I suspected.

I'm naked.

Chained.

Drugged.

The room is spinning, and my stomach is ready to hurl. The drugs haven't left my system. Elias took all the precautions, using heavy chains to tie me to the wall and stripping off my clothes. The room looks like a dungeon, and my cell is meant to be unbreakable for their worst enemies.

There are metal bars surrounding me and then a thick wall and door surrounding the bars. I glance around the room, looking for cameras I'm sure are there to keep a constant watch on me.

My heart starts speeding, and sweat pours from my brow. This was always the risk I took in this game—someone could be clever enough to outsmart me, and I would lose. Unlike the guys, losing doesn't mean death for me. I'll be violated in the worst way, and to me, that's worse than death.

You've been in situations like this before. This is what I trained you for. You won't fail, Kek's voice penetrates my fear.

I can't break literal metal. I can't break free of the drugs. I'm not strong enough.

I can hear Kek's vicious chuckle in my head. It's a haunting sound that both comforts me and fills me with dread.

If you fail, what was the point? Of my training? Of my death? Of your life? Of everything? You can't fail.

I can't fail.

He's right.

It will all be for nothing if I fail now when we are so close to the end.

What do I do?

You take a deep breath. Calm your fucking heart, your breath, your spinning head—everything needs to become still.

Right, breathe.

I close my eyes, blocking everything out as I take a breath and then another and another.

Everything slows. Everything stills.

And then I open my eyes.

Elias is staring back at me, watching me from the shadows like the coward he is. I can barely make him out.

"Why are you hiding? You had your men drug me, tie me in chains, and you're still afraid of me?" I taunt.

Elias takes a step forward from the shadows. "Just giving the drugs time to work their way out of your system. I don't want to fuck a corpse."

"Unlock the chains, and you won't be fucking a corpse." *You won't be fucking anything.*

He cocks his head as he studies me. "You shouldn't resist. The sooner I do this, the sooner this can all be over, and you can go back to a life of luxury and protection."

"I don't want that. I can take care of myself, thank you."

He grins. "It doesn't look like it from where I'm standing. You were far too easy to kidnap."

"Then why did it take fifty men?"

"You can never be too cautious. You're my future wife, and soon, you'll be carrying my future child. I had to do everything to protect you. I didn't want you to get hurt."

"Raping me is hurting me," I bite back.

"I'm sorry, Princess. If we had more time, I'd wine and

dine you first. But you'll realize when this is all over that I was right. I'm the only man you want to marry, and you'll be happy with me."

I laugh at the absurdity. "I will never be happy with a man who takes what he wants from me without my permission."

He studies me a minute. "Maybe I should sedate you so you won't remember."

I don't have a smart comeback. Drugs are the hardest thing for me to beat. But if he does inject me more, I'll have to do my best. I won't fail. I won't let him touch me.

He starts removing his jacket. "Don't worry; it will only be this way one time. Tomorrow I'm flying in a fertility specialist. From there, it will all be needles and IVF and anything that gives me the best chance of getting you pregnant this cycle."

"Then why fuck me now?"

"Because I want to increase my odds."

I shake my head with a grin. "No, you're afraid I'll escape, or someone better than you will kidnap me before tomorrow. You think this might be your only shot to get me pregnant, so you're taking it."

He frowns; I've guessed correctly. His eyes turn wild, on the verge of losing control.

I take another deep breath, calming myself.

And then he's in front of me—touching me, trying to grab my throat.

It's always the throat with men who need control—always about trying to cut off my oxygen, my ability to breathe, think, exist. I'm ready, though. I've prepared my entire life for moments like this. I won't fail.

Elias has one hand on my throat and the other on his pants. He's trying to hurriedly get his pants off so he can thrust inside me and show me how much of a man he is, show me how much power he holds over me.

All of my urges tell me to fight, to try and stop him. That's how I win this fight, though, so I do the opposite.

With his head bowed as he fumbles with his pants, I kiss his forehead.

He freezes, confused about what I just did. Slowly, he looks up at me. I lick my lips, although I'm barely able to get enough oxygen in my lungs with his tight grip.

My lips beckon him to me; he's unable to resist. He doesn't speak—I'm not sure he can right now anyway.

Then he's close enough so my tongue can touch the corner of his mouth. I refuse to kiss him, but teasing to get what I need from him—that's different.

He leans into the touch of tongue against his skin, releasing his grip on my neck enough for me to lick up his jawline. His eyes drift close, and I nudge his head, getting him into the perfect position. Slowly, I move my tongue further up his jawline.

I feel his erection between my legs, and I try not to cringe. I try not to think about how close I am to failing. I do what I have to by pretending I want this, by seducing him with the only part of my body I can control at the moment.

He tilts his head, and my tongue finally makes its way to his ear. I take my time, licking around the outer shell, getting him completely under my control.

Then I bite down—hard.

His high-pitched scream is exactly what I expected. He's a weak coward, terrified of a little pain.

I don't have much time before his men will notice, so I have to do this quickly.

"Key," I say through my gritted teeth, his earlobe still between my teeth.

He flails around, trying to push me off, but I just bite down harder.

"You fucking bitch. Let me go!"

"No! Key or I bite your ear off."

He groans as I clamp down harder.

I just need to get one chain undone—one limb free, and then I'll be able to break free. I hear footsteps above us—I don't have much time left, so I bite down harder and the taste of blood fills my mouth.

"Key," I growl.

Slowly, Elias reaches into his pocket and pulls out a key. He reaches up and puts it in my hand.

"Release me," he commands.

I let him go at the same time he releases the key.

He scrambles back a few feet, acting like I just shot him instead of barely biting him—wuss.

But I don't focus on him. I concentrate on undoing the chain at my wrist. I fumble once, but the second time I get the key into the hole.

The footsteps grow louder, but I don't see anyone coming down the stairs yet. I still have time.

I get my left arm undone.

I grin.

Quickly, I work on unlocking the other chains. By the time I've freed myself of every chain, there are still no men running down the stairs.

Odd.

"Your security team really sucks," I say.

Elias frowns, looking at the door behind him. He locked it when he came in, so I doubt he can just leave.

I'm still naked, but I don't care. I'm about to kick his

ass for touching me. For thinking he could take from me, for his slimy penis touching my body in any way.

He's still gripping his ear like I almost cut off a limb. His limp dick is barely poking through his jeans. Despite what just happened, the gleam in his eyes says he thinks he still has me. He thinks he can overtake me himself, or he'll have time to call down his men to restrain me.

I let him think that. I let him think he's about to get payback for making his ear bleed. His lobe is dangling, barely hanging onto the rest of the ear. I might have gone a little too far. Then again, he deserves to never be able to hear again.

Or see.

Or touch.

Or breathe.

He charges toward me at the speed of a raging bull. He reaches into this pocket at the last second, and I see the glint of a blade.

But he won't be touching me with that knife.

I wait until the last second. I let him get as close to me as I dare, and then I make my own move.

I evade him and grab his wrist, twisting the knife around until it drives into his stomach. The move is quick, and it takes him a second to register the pain before dropping to his knees like he's dying.

I doubt he's dying. The knife isn't that big, and he's barely bleeding. But he's groaning like death is seconds away.

It should be. I should end him.

Suddenly I feel familiar feelings of goosebumps on my arms and my speeding heart. I decide I have more important things to deal with than this man.

I lean down to get one last final word into his broken

ear. "I'm letting you live, but only so I can torture you the rest of your life. Don't ever come near me, touch me, or even try fuck me against my will ever again. In fact, don't touch any women ever again. If you do, I'll be the one doing the kidnapping next time. And I'll enjoy ripping you apart limb by limb. Do you understand?"

Elias wheezes.

Huh, maybe I did puncture a lung?

I examine him closer and realize there is no way I punctured a lung; the wound is far too low.

I reach into his pocket and pull out his phone. "Call for help. You won't die tonight, but I'd sleep with one eye open if I were you."

I walk away toward the cell entrance, and the outer stone door slowly opens until only the metal bar door separates me from freedom.

Beckett is standing on the other side of the bars. His eyes are locked on my eyes, but they slowly start drifting down, taking in my naked body. There's heat behind his gaze. He may be checking to see if I have any injuries or for evidence of what Elias has done to me, but he can't hide the heat in his eyes.

"You have a wife. You shouldn't be here," I say, crossing my arms and at least blocking some of his view of my bare breasts.

He chuckles. "Doesn't mean I can't look at a beautiful naked woman in front of me. Odette won't be upset with me for just looking."

"What are you doing here? Saving me, Hero?"

"No, I've learned my lesson where saving you is concerned. You're far better at it than I am."

"Then what are you doing?"

"Kidnapping you." That's when I see the others behind him—Ryker, Hayes, Gage, and Lennox.

I shake my head, and my eyes glisten with a taunt. "Go ahead and kidnap me. But take a close look at what happened to the last guy who tried. That's your fate."

10

BECKETT

HER THREAT IS music to my ears. Whatever happened here, she'll get over it. Any trauma from this place that won't destroy her if she's able to make threats like that.

That's all I want for her—a life free of the traumas of her past. A life where she can feel fulfillment. A life where she can one day find happiness.

Elias is lying on the floor, barely moving like he's already dead. He was brave to be the first to kidnap her, but it was a foolish move that will ultimately lead to his death.

"You going to make this easy? At least, until we get out of the house? We've taken out most of Elias's men, but we don't know what other security he has," I say.

Ri smiles at me. "When have I ever made anything easy for you?"

I grin back—still so feisty and full of life. I don't think anything will ever bring her down. I yearn for her, for the strength she contains, for her will to live and shine above everything else.

"Would you at least like clothes? Or should we kidnap you while you're still naked?"

Ri looks behind me to where the others stand gazing at her. I try to ignore the fact that they've all fucked her, and one of the lucky bastards will get to marry her.

I try to keep my rage and jealousy in check, but I'm sure it's all over my face. How long can I keep up the ruse that I love Odette, not Ri? Somehow I have to manage until I figure out how to take down Odette or until Ri is married.

"No, I don't think I'd like clothes. My body is a good distraction," Ri says.

Jesus.

She's right, but my job is hard enough trying to protect her. I don't need her naked body teasing me to make it even more difficult.

There are five of us and only one of her, but she could take us all down. She'll only go with us if she wants to, but I'm not sure if she does. I'm not sure of her motives at all. It seems like she's going along with her father's plan. She's not really fighting it, which is strange in and of itself.

I glance back to the guys, readying them for what we are about to do. They all give me a slight nod. I turn around to face Ri again and unlock the cell's inner metal door.

Here goes nothing.

We all push inside the small cell. It makes my stomach curl at the thought of what could have happened if Ri couldn't save herself. Even with how strong she is, it's clear she came very close to having everything taken from her. There is still the tiniest hint of fear in her eyes at what she could have lost in this dank cell.

We all draw our weapons even though none of us will

be using them against her, at least not to seriously hurt her. We won't even mark her skin. None of us can stand to hurt her.

She looks amused at the gun in my hand, raising her eyebrows. "You're going to shoot me if I don't go with you?"

"Maybe."

She glances quickly around the room, taking in the guns and knives drawn in everyone's hands.

We slowly surround her and then start inching closer to her. She doesn't seem fazed. She's been trained for years how to get out of situations like this, so I know it won't work.

Feigning bored, she waits for us to get within striking distance and then attacks. Hayes and Gage are the first to lose their guns. She kicks them out of their hands before they have a chance to even touch her.

Lennox grabs her wrist and holds his knife up to her throat. She quickly knocks his knife out of his hand and tosses it in Ryker's direction. It's a lazy throw, not one actually meant to hit him.

"Aw, come on, Princess, your aim is better than that," Ryker teases.

She smirks back. "Why are all the men around me so eager to die?"

"Oh, are you going to kill us, Princess? It doesn't seem like it. If you were going to, we'd already be on the ground next to Elias here moaning and taking in our last breaths," I say.

She lunges for me at the same time the guys move in. I aim my gun at her and fire, but not before she knocks the firearm away.

A loud groan ricochets around the room, far louder than the pathetic moaning still coming from Elias.

Ri turns and sees Hayes collapsed on the floor, gripping his chest. Ri falls to her knees as Hayes's eyes roll back in his head.

"Hayes!" she screams, putting her hand over his chest to stop the bleeding. "Hayes, hold on. Just hold on."

Tears are threatening her eyes as she turns to me. "Call for help!"

She immediately goes back to him, trying to apply more pressure, but the bleeding doesn't ease.

It's then I look to the others and nod.

We all descend on her—grabbing her arms and legs to start tying them behind her body.

"What are you doing? Save Hayes! I'll go with you willingly; just save Hayes!" Ri screams.

Only once we have her secured does Hayes open his eyes and stand up.

Her mouth drops as she stares at him. "You're—you're okay. But—"

"Sorry, Princess. We knew the only way to get you was to play to your weaknesses. I was voted most charming and the man we thought you'd care most about if I pretended to die," Hayes says.

Gage rolls his eyes. "He's just the best actor."

Hayes pulls out the fake blood to show her the truth. I didn't accidentally shoot him.

She slowly looks between us all with a wicked grin. "You cruel bastards."

We drive all night until we cross the border into Canada. Ryker found a large, secluded place in Toronto to give us some space and time alone with Ri. Ryker says it's completely secured. We rented a camper van, and each took turns sleeping.

Ri slept the entire time while someone also stood guard over her. The watch was more because she could escape at any second than because we were afraid someone was going to kidnap her.

Despite everyone sleeping most of the night in the van, everyone is exhausted when we arrive. Together, we carry Ri into the house covered in blankets. We never did convince her to put on clothes. She'll probably spend the entire time here naked just to spite me.

The house is a massive old stone exterior with modern interior renovations.

"This way," Ryker says, leading the way.

Gage, Lennox, Hayes, and I all follow, carrying Ri in our arms. To our surprise, she doesn't fight us. She lets us carry her, even though she's finally awake. She's probably as exhausted from the road trip as the rest of us.

Ryker leads us to the center of the house. "I picked this one because it has the least amount of windows. The walls are literally made of stone, practically bulletproof, but the inside is modern with a full security system."

"I'll get on updating the security system right away," Gage says as we enter the most central room in the house —it only has one door and no windows. The room has two couches, a bookshelf, and a grand piano in the corner. It will do perfectly until I can talk some sense into Ri.

We set Ri down on one of the couches. She doesn't say anything. She doesn't try to leave immediately.

"Leave us," I say to the others.

They nod, and everyone but Hayes leaves quickly. He lingers for a second, his eyes downcast and his movements heavy. "I'm really sorry, Ri. I didn't want to hurt or scare you."

She smiles weakly. "I know, Hayes. I'm just glad you're alive."

"I always knew you liked me the most." He winks at her.

"Get out of here so I can kick your boss's ass."

He laughs and then jogs out, the door locking behind him on the way out. Then it's just Ri and me.

I pull out a knife as I inch closer to remove the rope still tied around her wrists and ankles.

She stares at me with weary eyes as she watches me kneel in front of her. She doesn't budge as I cut the rope from her wrists and then ankles.

I wait for the punch, the kick, the threat—nothing comes. She doesn't move except to lift her blanket higher over her shoulders.

I stand.

"You going to rape me?" she asks with a hint of teasing in her voice.

"Why would I need to do that? If I wanted you, I could have you willingly." I lick my lips and watch as her mouth waters at the sight, proving my point.

She scoffs. "I would only let you touch me to get you close enough to castrate you."

I walk over and sit down on the couch opposite her. It seems like we are going to have a long conversation, and I'm not going to stand the whole time. It truly feels like we are on opposite sides, battling it out as we face each other.

I look her up and down. "Maybe I already got you pregnant. We've fucked several times since your birth control was removed. There's a good possibility I've already won the game."

"So cocky. But no, I'm not pregnant."

"I think you should pee on a stick since you aren't exactly trustworthy at the moment."

"If I am pregnant, it doesn't mean that you're the father."

I glare at her. "You haven't fucked any other man but me. The guys pleasured you, but they didn't fuck you. And you wouldn't have let anyone else go near you."

She bats her eyelashes at me. "You have no idea what I've done when we aren't together, just like I don't know what you've done. Don't act like you know me when you don't."

"I do know you, just like you know me," I say before I can think better of it. Ri knows me better than anyone, which is why I'm surprised she hasn't seen my true feelings for her yet.

"So, what's your plan? You're going to impregnate me to win? I don't think your dear wife will be okay with you fucking me and me carrying your firstborn child."

"I'll handle Odette. She knows I have to go to great lengths to win the game. All she cares about is that I win and survive. She'd much rather I cheat on her and live than be loyal to her and die."

"You're going to need some major marriage counseling after this is all over."

I chuckle. "Probably. But the state of my marriage isn't what I brought you here to talk about."

"What do you want to talk about?"

"I want to give you as much choice in your future as possible. We'll figure out what it means to win or lose later." I take a deep breath because her answer to the next question is going to hurt. "I want to know who you want. Do you want to marry Ryker, Lennox, Gage, or Hayes?"

11

RI

"Do you want to marry Ryker, Lennox, Gage, or Hayes?"

Beckett thinks I have a choice, a say in my own fate. I guess I do, just not in the way he thinks.

My mind is still spinning with their ploy to get me here. It was a smart move to play on my emotions, my feelings for Hayes. I care for him like a brother, and thinking he was dying in front of my eyes was terrifying.

But I shouldn't have reacted that way. I've let my emotions cloud my judgment for far too long.

I sit on the couch opposite Beckett. It feels like we're squared off for a fight, except I'm naked. He's leaning back casually on the couch; his leg crossed over the other knee while he casually waits for me to tell him which of his friends I want to marry.

Why is Beckett trying to help me?

He says he doesn't love me, that he loves Odette.

Is he that worried about losing? Does he really think I'd let him die?

Or is he doing this because even though he doesn't love me, our friendship is real?

"Since three out of the four are not eligible, I don't think it really matters," I say.

"Let me handle the details. For now, just dream. Tell me who you'd choose to spend your life with if given a choice."

Just dream—that's not something I can do. My entire life has been a nightmare.

If I answer honestly, I would choose Beckett. He's my equal, but I have to stop with my emotions and think logically. Dreams and emotions are what have gotten me into this mess.

"I can't dream. I have to be logical," I answer.

Beckett frowns. "Fine. Then logically, who would you choose?"

I just stare at Beckett and pull the blanket tighter around my body. I can't imagine choosing one of them. I can't imagine choosing anyone.

"We aren't leaving this room until you start talking."

That's not really a punishment. It means that reality can be put off for a few more days. It means I get to spend more time with Beckett in this fairytale.

We stare at each other, neither of us speaking. His gaze is warm and comforting, even when he's trying to force me to talk to him. He's begging me to tell him how he can help me; I can see the desperation in his eyes. And yet, I won't give him the answer he wants.

We sit.

We stare.

A silent standoff.

There's a knock on the door, and even then, we don't tear our eyes from each other.

"It's been a few hours; I thought you might want food and drink," Hayes says, bringing in a loaded tray.

We don't look at him. We don't speak to him. We only continue to stare at each other.

He sets the tray down on the coffee table between us.

"Really? You're not even going to talk to me?" Hayes asks as he tries to squat down between us to block our views, but we both crane our heads and continue to stare at each other.

Hayes sighs. "Fine, ignore me. I didn't slave away cooking you a gourmet meal of steak, crab cakes, and a side of asparagus for the last two hours or anything," he mumbles under his breath as he walks away. He pauses at the door, mumbling something else I can't make out before finally locking the door again.

"Poor Hayes," I finally say.

Beckett breaks out laughing as he grabs the bottle of red wine and starts pouring it into two glasses.

I take a deep breath, taking in the smell of the food. "It smells delicious."

"As you know, Hayes is an excellent cook. I'm sure it tastes as good as it looks."

We both reach for our own plates. I settle mine on my lap while Beckett balances his on his knee.

Steak isn't the easiest thing to eat without a table to eat at, but Hayes did leave us each a knife.

I grab the fork and knife. "Do you think Hayes is trying to start something?" I twirl the knife around in my hand.

Beckett chuckles. "Probably, but the food is too good not to eat first." He pops a bite of steak into his mouth and then moans in delight. It's a seductive sound meant to rattle me. I won't let him shake me.

I cut into my own steak and take a bite. As I do, I realize Beckett wasn't faking moans to drive me mad. He was making delighted noises because he couldn't resist. The sound that leaves my throat is primal and deep too.

"You're going to be the death of me," Beckett says.

I look at him and see darkness in his eyes. It's a lustful look he shouldn't have, not when he's married. Not when he's in love with another woman.

He's a conundrum I can't understand. Just like Beckett wants answers before we leave this room, so do I.

My main question is who does Beckett love? Or does he love anyone at all?

Even though it's not the smart move, I let myself enjoy every bite of food, every drop of wine that touches my lips. The sounds that leave me are not something I can control. I let myself feel every emotion, possibly for the last time.

When I've finished my plate of food and curled up on the couch with my wine, I finally feel the heat of Beckett's stare.

"You are impossible," he says, his eyes perusing my body.

I glance down as I realize the blanket has pooled at my waist, and I'm naked from the top-up. The way Beckett looks at me makes me never want to put clothes on again.

It has to be my imagination. He loves Odette. I heard his speech. I've seen them together. This is just a dream.

I stand up, letting the blanket fall all the way to the floor.

He swallows hard at the sight of me. His body tenses, and I swear I see a bulge in his pants.

He wants me.

I lick my lips, letting him know that I, too, want him.

He stands to move closer to me, I think. He wants to touch me, to possibly try and fuck me.

His hand reaches out, and he touches my cheek.

I close my eyes, leaning into his touch.

And then he's gone.

The door slams behind him on the way out.

I smirk. He may have succeeded in kidnapping me, but I just won our first battle. I drink down the rest of my wine.

I plan on winning a lot more.

12

BECKETT

I'M SO FUCKED.

So fucking fucked.

I slam the door behind me as Lennox jumps up from his seat with raised eyebrows.

"You okay?" he asks.

"No, I'm not fucking okay. The woman I love is probably going to marry you while I'm stuck married to a monster for the rest of my life."

I punch the wall just to feel something other than my unending lust for Ri. My knuckles redden but don't break. It's not enough to take me out of myself.

I punch again, but Lennox grabs my arm, stopping me.

I growl at him, but he doesn't let go.

"I need to talk to everyone." I start walking down the hallway. "Now."

"But Ri—"

"Ri won't leave that room, trust me." She's too intent on seducing the truth out of me.

Lennox stifles a chuckle as he follows me into the main living area of the house.

I march into the living room, where Ryker is stretched out on a couch. Lennox goes in search of Gage and Hayes.

Ryker's eyes widen as he looks at me. "She take your balls already?"

"Don't start," I grumble.

He grins as he sits up. The others make their way into the living room, sitting down on various pieces of furniture.

I stare at the four of them. Ri will be married to one of them in a month's time if I don't figure out a solution.

But I need to accept that reality. I need to help Ri choose; it's the most likely outcome.

"I'm in over my head," I say finally, letting my head fall back against the couch.

"No kidding," Gage says while the others chuckle.

I lean my head up and glare at them all. "None of you are helping."

"Well, we can't have that. What do you suggest we do?" Lennox says with a coy smile.

"Help me solve two problems at once."

Hayes raises his eyebrows. "Which are?"

"I need to find out Odette's plan. I need to find a way to take her down without hurting Ri."

They all nod back at me.

"And I need to find out who Ri would choose among you four if I fail and can't marry her myself."

No one responds to that.

I sigh and stand up, knowing I need their help and they'd rather be anywhere else, discussing anything else.

"I need two of you to go back to Chicago. I need you to spy on Odette. I need you to figure out who she told about Ri. I need to know everything about her plan —everything."

I run my hand through my hair as I stop pacing. "And I need the other two here with me, talking to Ri and trying to convince her to pick you. She has to pick. I can't keep her safe here forever. The faster one of you can charm her, the faster she'll be safe."

Silence meets me.

I stare down each of them individually. Ryker just narrows his eyes at me. Gage looks away. Hayes pouts in disbelief. And Lennox gives me a disappointed shake of his head.

"If anyone has anything to say about my plan, now is the fucking time!" I growl.

They all look at each other as if having a secret conversation without me. It's annoying as fuck.

"Speak!" I snap.

Lennox is the one who finally speaks. "The four of us should all go back."

"What? Why? If Ri tries—"

"She won't run. You said it yourself. She's too curious and wants this settled as much as any of us do. If she is to choose one of the four of us, then you two need to work out your shit. She will never marry any of us as long as she thinks there's still hope that you love her."

I frown, but I understand. I just don't know what to do.

"You aren't one to give up so easily. We will all return and devote all of our efforts to figuring out Odette's plan. We'll find out who she has told about Ri, and we'll find a way to stop Odette before the game is over. As much as any of us would love to marry Ri, we would never be able to enjoy it with you glaring at us every chance you get."

I look from Lennox to the others. "Odette is a ruthless woman. I don't understand why she's so focused on power, on going to war, on staying married to me. She will threaten you, and she has the entire Retribution Kings willing to do her bidding. If she realizes what any of you are doing, she will have you killed. That's something I'm not willing to risk."

"Odette doesn't have the entire Retribution Kings at her bidding. At least not the most handsome ones," Hayes says, standing.

"Or the smartest ones," Gage says, rising.

"Or the strongest ones," Lennox says, standing.

"You'll also have the help of my men as well. We can take down Odette," Ryker says, standing next to the others.

"Soon, you'll get your happily ever after. Just don't kill each other before we get back," Hayes teases.

If only it were that simple, but they give me hope I don't deserve. This hope is going to come crashing down and destroy me.

13

LENNOX

THE PLAN IS SIMPLE—GO back and give no clue as to where we've been or what Beckett's plan is. That's easier said than done. None of us trust anyone in the Retribution Kings anymore, and Odette is going to be suspicious as hell, but we have to try. Beckett's happiness, and ours, depends on it.

As much as I and the others care for Ri, she's not ours. She hasn't given us her heart. She's not our match—she's Beckett's.

Any one of us would marry her if we had to in order to protect her. We would try our best to make her happy, but we could never make her happy like Beckett could.

Beckett is our boss, but he's also our friend. We will do whatever it takes to give him his life back.

While Ryker is checking in with his men, the three of us are regrouping at our Chicago hotel.

"What's the plan again? I think we should stay as far away from her as possible—do some snooping or spy work instead," Hayes says as we walk down a hallway.

"The best way to uncover Odette's plan is to get close to her. Get her drunk or something to divulge her secrets. She's our best chance; we don't even know who else to start with," I say.

"I agree. We get to Odette. We've known her all our lives. We grew up with her. We used to be friends. We know her better than almost anyone. We can get her to talk," Gage says.

"Exactly, we know her better than anyone. You're both forgetting how annoying, self-righteous, and vicious she is, though," Hayes says.

"I don't remember her being anything but sweet, kind, and caring," Gage frowns.

Hayes laughs. "That's because she liked you. She hated me. She thought I wasn't smart enough to be friends with her brother. She teased me endlessly."

"And you teased her right back," I say.

"This will get us nowhere," Hayes says.

"You don't know that. We have to try everything unless you are volunteering to marry Ri and face her and Beckett's misery for the rest of eternity," I say.

"We need her to think we hate Beckett; we're angry and upset that Caius died. He was one of us, our closest friend. We can say we're playing double agents, pretending to be on Beckett's side when really we are on hers. Let's convince her we need to know her plan so we can help her," Gage says.

"Good thinking," I say as I knock on Odette's door.

"It's not going to work," Hayes mumbles under his breath.

I shoot him a glare, and he shuts his mouth just as Odette opens the door.

"What are you doing here? Where's Beckett?" she asks, standing in her robe.

"We're here to talk to you and make sure you're protected," I say.

"Protected? I'm pretty sure you are the ones I need protecting from."

I ignore her and push my way into her hotel room. The others follow me.

Odette follows me. "Where is Beckett?"

"He has to finish playing the game. If he doesn't, they'll kill him."

She sighs. "And when will the game be over?"

"A month, most likely," Gage answers.

"I have to be without Beckett for an entire month?"

"Yes," Hayes answers.

"Luckily, you get the three of us in the meantime," I say, flashing her wistful smile.

"Get out," she grumbles, not even wanting to hear us out.

Hayes gives me a look as if to say, 'I told you so.'

"You want to take down Beckett?" I ask, and she pauses, turning back around to face me. "Then let us help you."

She narrows her eyes as I stand and approach her.

"We know the truth—Beckett killed Caius in cold blood. We want revenge, same as you."

"There's just one little problem." She pauses, her finger working its way down my chest. "I don't want revenge against Beckett."

I frown.

"Then what do you want?"

She smirks. "Right now? I want you all to leave."

Then she walks into the bedroom and slams the door.

Hayes snickers, resting his arm on the back of the couch. "That went well."

I look to Gage. "Now what?"

He shrugs. "Get her drunk or…"

"Or?" I ask.

"Or play rock, paper, scissors to see which one of us tries to seduce her," Gage answers.

"Nah, I'm out of here," Hayes says.

I stare at the door, knowing one of us needs to at least try. We need to try everything. That's what being a Retribution King is really about. It's not about revenge and murder. It's not about payback. It's about being loyal to those you consider family and friends. We have to try everything to help Beckett.

I stare at the door. "No need. I'll sacrifice myself."

"Thank god," Hayes mumbles.

Even Gage says, "Good luck."

Then they both leave, walking out of the room.

Fuck, what have I gotten myself into?

I have no idea what I'm doing, but I have to figure out a way to get through to Odette and get her to trust me.

I walk into the kitchenette and grab a bottle of champagne, popping the cork. I would love something stronger, but this is all I find, so it'll have to do.

Maybe I should wait until tomorrow? I can wait for her to have had more time to realize that we are on her side.

No, we are running out of time. And giving her any time to think is just letting her plan and scheme to find more ways to attack Beckett.

It has to be now.

And if this plan fails, then we try again and again and again. We cannot fail.

For Ri's sake.

For Beckett's.

For our own.

We are a family, and I will not let anyone destroy it—especially not when Beckett is so close to happiness. Gage, Hayes, and I may never find a love like theirs. We may never have a chance for that kind of happiness, but dammit, I'm not going to let Beckett squander his future because of his fear of losing Ri.

I knock on Odette's bedroom door.

I don't expect an answer.

But a moment later, she slowly opens it with a half-smirk on her face. Her hair was up before, but it's now down in loose waves.

"I figured you'd be the one they'd send," she says.

"What do you mean?"

"You were always the leader, even when my brother tried so hard to be it. You were the responsible one, the one that carried the weight of the group on your shoulders. If Hayes got high and failed a mission, you took the blame. If Gage took apart a computer and couldn't put it back together, you said it was you. You're always cleaning up everyone's messes. It doesn't surprise me you're the one still here, trying to convince me of whatever scheme you've concocted."

She's right. I'm the one who always takes the blame. It's why I'm so cynical most of the time.

"I just came here to drink and do my job," I say, holding up a glass of champagne.

"Which is?"

"I told Beckett I'd keep an eye on you. I have to have something to report, so here I am."

She snatches the bottle of champagne from my hand as she turns away. She walks back into her bedroom and sits down on the edge of her bed before taking a long sip directly from the bottle.

I lean against the doorframe, trying not to be too obvious. She was always a talker when she drank, so hopefully, that hasn't changed.

She holds up the bottle. "Trying to get me drunk, so I'll talk?"

I frown. Apparently, I'm too obvious.

I walk over to her, take the bottle from her hand, and take a long drink.

She cocks her head to the side as she looks up at me. "You can't trick me, Lennox. I've known you all for years. None of you have ever liked me."

"Hayes least of all."

She grins at that. "Then I did my job well."

"Maybe we did our jobs well too. Caius wouldn't let any of us like you even if we wanted you." I chuckle. "He threatened us plenty of times with murder if we so much as touched you, let alone fuck you. He was beyond protective of you."

Our eyes meet. "Maybe now that he's gone, it's time to protect you in a different way. I know your relationship with Beckett is strained. But if you tell me that Beckett should live, then I'll let him live. Just let me help you with whatever you have planned."

She snatches the bottle back and takes another gulp. I watch as the liquid goes down her throat. I try my best to seem attracted to her. I lock onto her luscious red lips like I want to kiss them, but all I want to do is tape them shut.

I let my gaze linger on her thin throat as she swallows slowly. But all I can think about is how I want to choke her for threatening Ri.

I lick my own lips and think of her naked in bed, trying

to seduce her with my gaze. But all I want is to torture her until I find out the information I need to help Ri.

I can't torture her, or she might set her plan into motion. Ri might die if I screw this up. Or Beckett might stay married to this monster forever.

Suddenly, she laughs. Throwing her head back, she laughs and laughs and laughs. She laughs so hard that tears drip out of her eyes. She falls back on the bed laughing, somehow keeping the Champagne bottle upright and not spilling a drop.

Her body trembles with laughter. Then the snorts start, followed by the hiccups.

"What am I missing?" I ask when it's clear she's not going to stop.

"You're a terrible actor, Lennox. I don't know what game you're playing. I don't know who you're loyal to, and I don't care, but please spare me your sexy eyes again. It just looks like you're constipated, not trying to seduce me."

"I'm not playing a game. I'm sorry if you don't find me attractive, but I've always found you attractive and—"

She makes a zipping motion with her fingers, and I stop talking, realizing I've failed. I'm going to have to try a different way to get information from her. Or I could let Gage try; Hayes would just end up killing her.

I'm not beyond trying torture. Beckett thinks if anything happens to her, the same or worse would happen to Ri, but I can't let Odette win. I'm a good friend, and I'd marry Ri if that is what everyone thought was best, but I don't plan on marrying, ever.

Everyone thinks I'm the one who always steps up, who takes on the responsibility when the others fuck up. But this time, I'm doing this for myself. As much as I like Ri, I can't get married.

Even though I may not believe in happily ever afters, Beckett and Ri make me believe that for some small percentage of people, the one percent of the one percent, they're real.

That tiny bit of hope is enough for me.

14

RI

I'M LYING on the carpet in the middle of the room, spread eagle when the door opens again. I don't move. I couldn't have planned this better myself, even though I was just getting comfortable on the floor.

I feel a lump of fabric hit my stomach.

I peel an eye open to look down and find a pile of clothes.

"Put them on," Beckett commands.

"You know, I'm really tired of your commands. If you want me to do something, you should ask. Otherwise, I'm just going to fight you."

Beckett grits his teeth as he stands over me, clearly on his last nerve with me already. This is going to be a long few days together if he's already riled up at me.

"Ri, will you please put on some clothes?"

"Thank you for asking, but no."

Beckett's glare turns downright diabolical. I'm pretty sure I'm about to find out if he has any real feelings for me right here, right now. If I live, then he does care.

I raise my eyebrows and grin up at him as he stands over me with a sigh.

"Can we at least sit on the couch?" he asks.

"You can. I'm going to lie right here."

"Why do you have to make everything so difficult?"

"Why do you have to make everything so boring?"

"I should just hire a doctor to shove some of everyone's sperm up in you, and whoever's sperm takes wins. Or he loses because he has to put up with you for the rest of his life."

He's grumpy today. Lack of sleep and being tortured by someone he can't have will do that to a person.

I sit up and grab the shirt on top and slowly put it on. I don't bother with the bra or panties or even pants. The shirt is the only compromise he's getting out of me.

"Better?"

"Yes, thank you," Beckett sighs as he sits down on the rug next to me. He doesn't lie back like I do, but I'm guessing this is his compromise.

He sits in silence for a minute while I continue to stare up at the ceiling, counting the dots on the popcorn ceiling like I would stars.

"Tell me who you think I should pick," I say suddenly.

Beckett looks over at me. "Why do you think I have any idea who you should pick?"

"Just humor me."

"I guess whoever was best in bed," he teases.

"Hayes wins then," I say.

He gives me a dirty look.

"What? You thought I was going to say you? Sorry, but Hayes is bigger, and he's a more selfless lover. You're far too selfish. I don't know how Odette puts up with you."

He growls. "I am not a selfish lover."

I laugh.

He falls back, exhausted with me.

I laugh harder.

Beckett is by far the best I've ever had, but I won't be admitting that out loud ever again, and definitely not to his face.

"Come on, give me your pros and cons list. Tell me why you think I should or shouldn't marry each of them," I say.

I need help. Beckett is off the table. I need to think of the others objectively, and Beckett can help with that. And his plan will work. If I want Lennox, Hayes, or Gage instead of one of the main four remaining, then Vincent would honor that if Beckett technically won.

Beckett puts his hand behind his head. "Who should I start with?"

"Gage."

"Well, the pros are Gage is the smartest. You would never have to worry about security with him. He would always have you covered. And he's good at keeping secrets."

"All good points. And cons?"

"Cons are he doesn't want to lead an organization. He's too quiet and possibly too nerdy for most of the men to take him seriously. He's too serious for you, and he's not in love with you."

I laugh at his last one. "Alright, Hayes next."

"Hmm, well, apparently, he's the best in bed. He's loyal to a fault. He's kind, sweet, charming."

"He's a good chef. I'd never go hungry."

"You'd never go hungry. And he's lovable, like a puppy. You'd laugh the most with him."

I nod, agreeing.

"But he's also the easiest to trick. You would spend as much time protecting him as he would protecting you. He's a pushover, and the Corsi men would eat him for dinner. And he's not in love with you."

I analyze everything Beckett said, and I know it to be true. Although he's the sweetest and easiest to love, I can't marry Hayes because he would be the worse protector. Gage remains in the running simply because he's a better protector.

"Okay, what about Lennox?"

Beckett takes a deep breath like this conversation is taxing him. "Lennox...where to start with him? He's a born leader. He's better at it than me, better Caius ever was. He's intelligent and level-headed. And he'd approach a relationship like a second job."

"But?"

"He's too serious, and he's always hated you."

"Hey, he doesn't hate me anymore."

"Still, he held a grudge against you, and that doesn't go away easily, even if it seems like it."

"Fine, point made."

"And if he leaves, there will be no one left to lead the other two."

"You wouldn't lead them?" she asks.

"Yes, I'm the leader of the Retribution Kings, but I mean the three of them specifically. I do my best, but he's known them the longest. He's who they depend on. And he's hiding something dark; I can tell."

"You're probably right. But then again, I'm guessing all of them have dark secrets."

"And he's not in love with you." Beckett's eyes meet mine, and I can see that's the most hurtful part for him to say. He desperately wants one of them to be in love with me. That would somehow make this all easier—if one of them just loved me or if I loved one of them.

I don't want to tell him it would actually make it much harder. Love clouds everything. I need to think logically about the man I'll spend the rest of my life with, and love has nothing to do with it.

"And Ryker?" he asks. "I've spent the least amount of time with him, but he's an excellent pick. Already a good leader. A good actor. He's already feared. You two have chemistry together. Maybe even more so than with the other three. I've seen it with my own eyes."

I blush at that.

"But the only way a man can act as cruel as Ryker is if he's experienced torture or has a small streak of vicious-ness inside him. He's the biggest wildcard. He'd protect you, but I'm not sure if he would challenge you. He'd put his men and empire above you. And—"

"And he's not in love with me," I say.

He nods.

"So, what do you think? You've heard my opinions; what are yours?" he asks me.

"I think any one of them could do the job, even with their faults. But I'm still not sure who the right guy is."

"How are you going to choose?"

"I don't know."

"Do you feel like you need to spend time with them? Should we form our own little game to see who knows you the best or who's the strongest or something?"

I laugh. "God, no, that's the last thing we should do." I smack Beckett. "Thanks for giving Vincent the idea of the game in the first place—just a brilliant idea," I say sarcas-tically.

"I stand by it. It's still a brilliant idea."

"How exactly? We've both almost died. Everyone who has lost has died even if they didn't deserve it. Two of my friends died. Caius died."

His face drops. "I'm sorry. I still can't get over Lucy and Kek—I'm sure I'll never know the full story on him, but I'm sorry that you lost him."

I sit up, hugging my knees against my chest.

Beckett slowly rises next to me, mirroring my moves.

"I still need to talk to Odette. Whether you love her or not, I need to know she can't hurt me. I need her to forget."

I expect Beckett to argue with me. I expect him to tell me to leave her out of it.

"I know. I'm working on it," is all he replies.

HAYES

I ALWAYS GET the worst jobs. I huff as I walk into the bar.

Okay, maybe that's not fair. Lennox spent the entire night with Odette, and judging by his grumpy mood this morning, he failed miserably at getting close to her.

Gage is too occupied playing spy by reviewing every security camera and trying to hack into the computers and phones of her and every other suspect in the Retribution Kings.

And I won't go near Odette unless we've agreed on the torturing her route. Then I'll be happy to coerce some information out of her.

Instead, I have this crappy job that definitely won't work. But as Lennox said, it's my turn to do something for once. He acts like I don't do any work, *but who do they ask when they want to eat? Me.*

I've barely sat down at the bar before I sense him.

"Ryker," I say with a genuine smile. "So glad you could make it."

"You didn't exactly give me a choice." He frowns as he sits down at the bar next to me.

It's a crowded bar. There are people sitting the entire length of the bar, and the bartender is overwhelmed, so it'll take a while to get anything to drink. But that's never stopped me before.

I reach over the bar and snap up two glasses and the closest bottle before quickly pouring the liquid into the glasses and putting the bottle back.

Ryker stares at me incredulously and sniffs the drink. "This smells horrible."

"Do you want a drink in the next hour? Then this is what you're getting."

He rolls his eyes. "Or I could go home where I'd find a lot better to drink there. Why are we in the most crowded bar in the city?"

He stares me down. "So I can't make a scene when you tell me whatever you're going to tell me."

I shrug as I take a sip of my drink before almost spitting it out. I must have picked a bottle of the cheapest tequila in the bar.

"Why am I here, Hayes?" Ryker asks again.

"We need your help with Odette."

"I've been helping. I've been using my own resources to look into her and surveil her. And I've come up with three guys who seem to be working with her—Stan, Keith, and Dominic. I should have contacted you guys sooner, but I wanted to be sure I didn't miss anyone. I—"

"Gage has already come to the same conclusion."

"Okay, so then why do you want to talk to me?"

"If it were as simple as just surveilling her, we'd already have taken the three of them out and brought Ri home. But it's not. Odette is far from simple. She's secretive, sly, and most of all, a liar."

Ryker frowns. "I still don't know what you want me to do about it."

"Lennox was our best chance of someone getting close to her. He failed. Gage is better behind a computer, and I can't stand the woman. So..."

"No," Ryker says before I even finish speaking.

"We have to try everything. We have too much history with Odette. But you—you have no history with her."

"So you want me to what—fuck her? Coerce her? Get her to divulge all her secrets to me just because I have a big dick and am good in bed?" He tosses back his drink. "You really think that a woman who is as sly as you say she is would so easily divulge her secrets to a stranger? Do you really think a woman who holds all her power from being married to Beckett would cheat?"

"We won't know until we try. You're charming. You got Ri to like you even though she loves Beckett. How is this any different?"

"It's different because I like Ri. This Odette seems like a pain in my ass."

"Just try; that's all we're asking. Try."

"No."

"Fine, then you'll marry Ri knowing she loves another man? Knowing you can never make her happy? Knowing she'll be miserable the rest of her life?"

Ryker glares at me, narrowing his eyes as he reaches across the bar and grabs the same cheap bottle of tequila. He pours himself another glass, tossing the liquid back before refilling his glass and taking another shot.

I have him. He'll do whatever needs to be done because he cares about Ri just like we do.

"I don't know what you expect from me. Odette isn't going to give me the time of day, but I do care about Ri—

enough not to marry her unless it's the only way to save her.

"Fine, I'll try for her. But I wouldn't hold my breath on the outcome. And I'd start planning a plan B."

I throw some money down, and we both walk out of the bar. "You are the plan B, and I'm not sure we have time for a plan C."

16

BECKETT

"She killed Lucy," Ri whispers.

I narrow my eyes but don't let any of my feelings out. I'm not sure where she's going with this. I'm not sure why she hasn't attempted an escape yet.

I don't know why she's sitting here so relaxed and acting like we are just two friends having a pleasant conversation. I've very skeptical. I'm pretty sure she has a plan, an angle; I just haven't figured out what it is yet.

"Odette—she killed Lucy," Ri says while watching my face closely, so I keep it as nonchalant as I can. I don't even speak.

I know Ri's right. Odette and Caius killed Lucy, but I don't know why. I don't know her motives except that she wants to hurt Ri, hurt me, hurt everyone in her life. I don't understand Odette, but hopefully, the guys are figuring it out.

I can't stay married to her forever, not when Ri walks this earth. I don't deserve her, but I want a real chance to fight for her, to be honest, tell her everything, and see how she feels.

Ri grits her teeth when I don't try to defend Odette or even disagree with her.

"Do you agree? Odette killed Lucy?"

I clear my throat, knowing she won't give up until I answer her. "Maybe. I don't really know. I wasn't there. You'd have to present the evidence against her for me to believe it. But Odette is a strong woman. She's capable of many things. She's capable of murder just like you are. And I'm sure if she did, she had her reasons."

"Unbelievable." Ri stands abruptly and starts pacing the room.

I remain seated on the floor. If I stand, I'll get worked up right along with her. I'll show my emotions, and I need to guard them carefully until Odette has been dealt with. Odette could have anyone prepared to hurt Ri. If I was Odette, it would be someone close to Ri.

Fuck, someone close to Ri. That would mean Gage, Hayes, or Lennox—even Ryker.

Fuck, fuck, fuck.

I can't trust any of them.

Ri tilts her head, noticing the anger rising in my chest. "How could you love her?"

I stand—it's a mistake. I know the second my blood rushes through my veins, but I can't help it. I'm too frustrated with myself for not realizing that one of them is most likely working for Odette. *But who?*

Ri moves in front of me, stepping into my space.

"How could you love her when she killed someone so innocent?"

"I doubt Lucy was innocent," I snark back.

Ri punches me—hard across the cheek. My head snaps to the side as the hit lands, and my eye feels like it's coming out of its socket. It's probably fair considering she just lost her friend, and I basically said she deserved it. But I'm not thinking logically. All I'm thinking about is how I fucked up.

"Lucy was my best friend, the only one who stuck by me. Don't you dare say Lucy wasn't innocent. She was the only person who ever cared about me. She didn't deserve to die!"

Ri charges at me.

I blink, still struggling to see out the eye she just clobbered, but I'm not going to let her hurt me without consequence. I attack at the same moment she does. Her hand flies to my face again, but I block her fist at the same time I knee her hard in the stomach, knocking the breath out of her.

She takes a step back, gripping her stomach and catching her breath. "I can't believe you just did that."

"No kidding, since it was such an obvious move, you should have easily blocked. It seems like you're letting your emotions get the best of you."

Her nostrils flare and her hands fist, ready to punch again.

"Why did Odette kill Lucy? If Odette is the love of your life, then she would have told you. You would have known. You would have been okay with it. Why did she do it?"

I shrug. "I don't know. Odette and I have this thing between us called trust. It's why we work. I don't question her every move, and she doesn't question mine. It's why you and I would never work. No trust between us."

"That I believe, but the other statement is just plain bullshit." Ri circles me, her fists up, ready for a fight. She throws a jab, I duck.

"Lazy punch."

I throw another kick. She avoids it easily this time,

rolling her eyes. "That was lazy." She throws out a combination of punches and kicks—this time stronger than before. I dodge most, but she gets a punch into my shoulder.

"You know what I think? I think she killed Lucy because she thinks Lucy knew something. She thinks Lucy knew her secrets and was willing to spill them, but I don't think Lucy deserved to die," she says.

"Any more than Caius deserved to die? Sometimes death is inevitable. Sometimes it's our destiny to die young," I reply.

"You're a fucking asshole. Is that why you love her? You two are evil fucks together?"

This time when she punches, she doesn't let up. I'm too riled up and focused on my own idiocy, so I instinctively punch right back, acting like she's my enemy instead of the woman I'd die for.

I hit her in the throat.

She retaliates with a kick to the groin.

Another punch to her stomach.

And then she gets one in my sternum.

We're both panting, frustrated as hell with each other. It's clear what her goal is—she's trying to push me to admit I don't love Odette.

But I won't slip up. I love Ri too much for that. I need her to think I'm head over heels about Odette, at least for a little longer. At least until I solve the mystery that is my wife.

She takes a step back. I take a step forward.

Another back.

Another forward.

And then my hands reach out to her. But instead of grabbing her throat or throwing another punch, my hand lands on her waist. She grips my shirt as she yanks me close.

We're still steaming mad, but there's also an undercurrent of lust that always exists when we're together.

I glare down at her.

She cocks her head back, licking her bottom lip seductively; she thinks this is where I'll break. With my hand on her hip bone, standing so close that we are breathing the same air, I'll give into my lust and kiss her.

I won't break. I can't. I have to remain strong to save her.

"I'm tired of your games, Princess."

"And I'm tired of yours," she hisses back.

"Then end this. Tell me who you want to marry, and this will all be over. We can go our separate ways and never see each other again." Just don't pick the man who is on Odette's payroll. Then you'll be in even more danger, and I'll never be able to keep you safe.

"How can you love her? She's a monster," Ri's voice breaks. Her eyes water as she thinks about her lost friend, probably also thinking about losing me.

I raise my hand, placing it under her chin so I can see all of her tears, all of her pain, all of everything I deserve to feel.

It ruins me seeing her like this—in so much fucking pain, pain I'm causing. But it's moments like this that I remember why even if I solve my Odette problem, it doesn't really matter. The other guys are better—kinder, sweeter, more compassionate. We've all killed, but so far, I'm the only one who has proven to betray her. I'm not the man for her. I never will be.

"We're all monsters. Love doesn't care if the person is a

monster or not; it just exists. Everyone deserves to be loved. I'm her person, and she's mine."

Ri's face falls in defeat.

"Plus, between Odette and me, I'm the bigger monster."

Maybe it's time I explain to Ri why.

17

RYKER

WHY AM I DOING THIS?

This is so stupid. It's not going to work. They couldn't get Odette to talk to them; she's not going to talk to me, a complete stranger.

I'm doing this because of Ri, because I love her.

I'm not in love with her. Although, I could easily fall for a woman like Ri if she wasn't already in love with another man.

For now, Ri's like the girl next door that I like to look after. The hot 'could kick my ass better than any man' girl next door. I'm not even convinced Ri needs my help.

I'm still in favor of Beckett just telling Ri the truth and them working together to get rid of Odette and any other attacks against them. But nobody listens to me outside of my own men. I'm ready for this to be all over so I can spend my time just doing my damn job instead of playing stupid games.

I'm staked out outside the Retribution Kings' office downtown. This is the office that handles what the world sees—the real estate and law offices that claim to make the millions while they're really smuggling drugs and weapons and every other criminal way they can make money.

I know Odette is coming. Hayes texted me her schedule, and this is where I agreed to try and meet her. Hayes didn't understand why I wouldn't try to run into her at the bar she frequents at night, but that's the worst place to try to pick up a woman who doesn't want to be hit on.

Her driver pulls up, and she steps out in a fitted black dress that covers her curves but is somehow still sexy as hell. She's clearly going for boss lady vibes with her attire all the way down to her black pumps and perfect blonde bun.

I start walking as soon as she opens the door into the office building. I'm several feet behind her, but I'll easily catch up. She can't take very big strides in her heels. Plus, I want to time it perfectly.

I enter the building behind her and flash the guard a fake badge as I follow her to the elevator banks. She steps into an empty elevator, and just as the door is about to close, I put my arm between the doors.

She has her phone out, typing away on it, but her eyes look up to flash me a death stare as my arm holds the door open, delaying her from getting to her meeting on time. She's about to be in for a rude awakening if she thinks five seconds is a delay.

I step on, and Odette goes back to typing on her phone as I hit the button for two floors below hers.

The doors close, and the elevator takes off.

I ignore her but don't take out my own phone. I just act completely disinterested, like her long legs, red lips, and heavenly perfume do nothing for me. If I didn't know who she was, I might want to hit on her just because I could.

She's not exactly my type, but she's hot, strong, and in charge. I can work with that.

She licks her lips and makes this soft purring sound, almost as if she needs the attention, thrives on it.

I ignore her harder, staring at the floor numbers as we rise, acting like they are far more interesting than her.

I can practically feel her pouting next to me as she holds her hand out next to mine, probably going for the casual move of letting our fingers brush together to see if there is any electricity between us.

I put my hands in my pockets, and her pout intensifies. It's adorable. I want to laugh at her, but it would ruin my act of not giving her any attention.

I don't think Odette would actually cheat on Beckett with me. I think too much is at stake for her to be seen as a cheater right now, but she's a woman used to being fawned over. I'm not that type of man, though. I only give someone attention if they deserve it, and Odette doesn't deserve it.

We get to the fifteenth floor, and the elevator stops, but the doors remain closed just like I planned.

She huffs, immediately annoyed, even though she has no idea how long this will last. She has no idea if it will last five seconds, five minutes, or five hours. For both our sakes, I hope I break her before we get anywhere close to the five-hour mark.

She stomps her foot down as she approaches the elevator panel. She presses the button for her floor incessantly, like that will somehow get the elevator button moving.

"Fine, I'll just take the stairs. I could use the exercise anyway." She presses the button for the doors to open, but they don't budge.

She stares at me incredulously, but I continue to ignore her. I don't show any displeasure or any emotion. She has no idea what's going on in my head.

"You're supposed to say I look great and don't need the exercise. That's the polite thing."

I can't help it; I chuckle at that. "Really? That's what you're mad at? I didn't tell you your ass looks good."

She gives me a scathing look as her blue eyes shoot daggers in my direction. She turns back toward the elevator panel and presses the help button.

Nothing happens.

Nothing is going to happen until I give the cue to get us moving again.

"What the hell? Why isn't this working?" This time she looks at me with slight panic in her eyes.

I don't respond.

"Hello! Are you are going to talk to me or try to fix this?"

I chuckle again. "I assumed your question was rhetorical. And I'm not an elevator technician. How would I know how to fix the elevator?" I raise my eyebrows.

"Because you're, you know..."

"Because I have a dick? Isn't that sexist?" I grin slyly at her.

She crosses her arms and sticks out her hips. "No, that's not sexist."

"Oh, so you're one of those women who believe that sexism only exists if it happens to the woman, not the man."

She bites her bottom lip, and I can practically see the steam coming out of her ears. I don't know if this is the right way to get her to talk to me or not, but I sure as hell know that flattery won't get me anywhere. And I'm quite enjoying arguing with her and teasing her, so I keep going.

"You're probably one of those stay-at-home husbands married to a woman who works all the time and brings home the dough while you sit on your ass and pretend to cook and clean, aren't you?"

I hold up my left hand. "Not married."

She narrows her eyes looking for a tan line.

"Fine. Boyfriend, fiancé, whatever."

"Nope, not currently in a relationship."

"Then, get over here and try to figure out how to work this damn elevator and stop acting like someone is going to be upset if you stand within a foot of me."

I take a step back. "Maybe I just don't want to help you. You seem like the uptight kind, and I'm more of a chill guy. I don't think we would work well together."

"I'm not asking you to marry me or even like me, just fix the damn elevator."

I take another step back until I feel the elevator wall behind me. I slide down to the floor until I'm sitting.

"What the hell are you doing?"

I close my eyes and stretch my legs out. "I'm waiting for the elevator technician to come and fix the elevator instead of having a coronary like some people."

She frowns. "Do you think this imaginary elevator technician will be coming soon?"

I shrug, not opening my eyes. "Maybe, maybe not."

"And that doesn't bother you, that you have no idea how long it's going to take for him to come? Don't you have something important to do?" She pauses for dramatic effect. "Oh, that's right. You don't work or do anything important. You mooch off your parents, most likely."

I chuckle. "You're really wound up; you know that? But if you must know, yes, I do have somewhere important to be. I just don't believe in getting worked up and anxious about things I can't change."

"How do you know you can't change things when you haven't even tried?"

"As I said, I'm not an elevator technician. I watched you press the buttons; they don't work. I might as well meditate or nap or do something useful."

She rolls her eyes at me and pulls her phone back out.

"Unbelievable, I don't have reception in here."

I can feel her eyes on me, and then she kicks my foot. "Hey you, want to try your phone and see if it has any reception?"

"I don't have a phone."

"Yes, you do; I can see it in your front pocket."

"What are you staring at my crouch for?" I smirk.

"You stared at my ass and tits; now we're even."

I laugh. "You're really full of yourself; you know that?" That's when I pretend to notice her ring for the first time.

"Especially for someone who's married," I say with a disapproving look.

"Like a guy like you cares that I'm married."

"A guy like me? What's that supposed to mean?"

"I don't know what you do, but it can't be important. You're not wearing a suit, your jeans are from Kohl's, your watch is a knock-off, and your shoes are covered in mud. You don't work in an office; you work in the field, which means you don't make much money, you didn't go to college, you're not that smart."

I raise an eyebrow and shake my head, disappointed in her. "So a guy like me would take any attention from a woman like you whether she's married or not? A guy like me has no morals and knows the only way he can ever fuck a woman like you is if she feels like cheating? Because what could I possibly offer a woman like you except a quick fuck?"

She shrugs. "I'm not wrong. You don't have enough money to satisfy me."

I let my eyes run up and down her body, evaluating her in the same way.

"Prada shoes, a designer dress, well-manicured hands. I get it; a girl like you takes a lot of money to be made beautiful every day."

She scoffs. "I'm beautiful without all of this."

I look at her in disbelief. "I doubt that, sweetheart. But you say I don't have enough money to be able to afford a date with you anyway."

"You don't. It's a fact."

"The problem is you don't know how to judge men. You think just because I don't wear an expensive designer suit that I don't have money. Honey, I have more money than you can dream of. Money I've earned with my hands, not in an office."

"Prove it."

"Why should I? I don't want to go on a date with you."

"Don't you? You should know I'm more than just a pretty face. I have plenty of power and money of my own."

"Good for you, but that's not what I look for in a woman."

"What do you look for?" she asks, far too curious.

Maybe I will be able to do this. I won't make her fall in love with me, but I can get her to go out with me long enough to learn some of her secrets. Or at least I could get her into her bed so I can explore her shit when she's asleep.

"A woman who doesn't care about my wealth, for one."

"You still haven't confirmed that you're wealthy."

I look up at the corner of the elevator and give a slight nod of my head, indicating we should move again. I have her captivated; that's all I can hope for.

The elevator starts moving again.

I stand up, but Odette holds her ground in front of me. We're face to face, exchanging oxygen with each other.

The door opens on my floor.

"This is my floor," I say.

"Uh-huh," she says, not able to get any other words out.

I put my hands on her hips.

She sucks in a breath as I lean in close like I'm about to kiss her. She licks her lips and then parts them, readying herself for a kiss.

Then I gently move her to the side and walk past her out of the elevator. I don't need to turn around to see if she's following me; I can hear her heels clicking on the ground as she does.

I grin like an idiot as I keep walking through the office floor. I stop suddenly, and she slams into my back. It amuses me to no end.

I turn and face her. "Can I help you?"

"You're one of them," she says suddenly like she's figured it out."

"Hmmm?" I play dumb.

"You're playing the stupid game to win the Rialta girl. You're an organized crime boss. You don't make money; you steal it."

I bow. "That's me, Ryker Parks. And you—you're no better than me. You married a boss and are manipulating him to try and start a war."

She glares at me.

I hold her gaze right back.

"I can't believe you manipulated me like that! You're just trying to fuck with my head, just like all the rest of them! You—"

I lean forward and press my lips against hers. It's a tame kiss for me, but I'm shocked to see how her lips feel against mine. My heart thumps wildly, and I feel warm and hot inside, something I haven't felt before.

It's probably just because I've been told how bitter and cold she is, so I was expecting her kiss to make me feel cold, not warm—that's all. There is nothing else to the kiss.

I pull away, and her lips stay puckered as if she was hoping for a longer kiss.

Her eyes land on mine, and finally, she says, "What was that for?"

I grin. "I needed to shut you up somehow."

Quickly, I walk away before she can truly process what happened. Hayes will be mad that more didn't happen, but if he wants this to work, I'm going to need to move slowly with her. If I push her too far, too fast, we won't get anything. I just hope Beckett's plan to stall gives me enough time to crack Odette and hopefully not fall victim to her schemes.

A chill runs through my body, one that unsettles me and makes me think that falling victim isn't what I should be worried about. I should be worried about a very different falling.

18

RI

I'M TRYING to push Beckett to break. I get close, but every time I do, he pushes me away—so close and yet so far.

I need to know for sure how Beckett feels. He's the best choice by a million miles. I suspect I know the truth, but if he is the best choice, the right choice, the only choice— then I need to hear it from him. He needs to be the one to say it. That's the only way I'll choose him.

I have to push him to his absolute limit because he thinks he's doing the right thing. While he's amazing for doing it, the best thing for him to do is tell the truth. Tell the truth, and then I can make the best decision for all of us.

We're still standing close, my back to a wall and Beckett's hand tucked under my chin. Tears water my eyes for everything I'm about to lose—I know my fate. I'll lose practically everything no matter what Beckett chooses, but I can help him pick the best option for him.

His eye is already swelling from where I hit him, and I'm sure my ribs are turning black and blue from where he got me. We are so volatile together. It might be better if we aren't in each other's lives anymore, but I have to be sure.

"You really love her?" I ask my question quieter this time. He's sick of me asking, but until I'm one thousand million percent sure, I won't choose anyone else.

He doesn't answer. He doesn't blink. He just stares at me.

"I just need to know the truth, whatever it is. I can take it. Please."

His teeth slowly scrape along his bottom lip. I'm not sure if I've pushed enough or if I've pushed too far, but it's not in my nature to give up. So I keep pushing, keep hoping he'll answer me.

"How can you love a woman who betrayed you? Who's trying to start a war with your brother? Your family?" I whisper.

My eyes glide back and forth over his, and I can see the darkness brewing there. I see the pain, the need to talk to me, but also the pull to keep everything inside, so it doesn't break him. I don't know why the truth would destroy him.

After everything I've seen him go through, I think it's impossible for him to break. He's stronger than he realizes. He can endure anything; I've seen him endure hell. Whatever is eating him up, he'll survive that too.

"We all need this to end. We need the games to end and the wars to hopefully stop before they start. But we can't do that until this game is over. I'm trying to decide, but I can't until I know the truth. Just tell me the truth, and then I can move on. No one else is here. There is nowhere else for us to go. Just be honest with me, Beckett. You owe me that."

He doesn't move for a heartbeat. I assume, once again, I'll get nothing real from him, nothing more than I've gotten every other time.

But then, his hand drops from my face, and he takes a step back.

"Do you want wine or something harder?" he asks.

I look at him in confusion.

"You want the truth? Then we're both going to need a drink."

"Wine, please." I'm afraid of anything stronger. He may need a drink, but I need to be sober, so my feelings don't affect my decisions. My emotions have always failed me.

Beckett nods and leaves the room.

I pace for a second, full of nervous energy, but then decide to just sit. I don't want to scare Beckett off now that he's decided to talk, and my nervous energy might do just that.

I sit, but soon I realize my legs are bouncing up and down.

Jesus, I'm a mess.

I'm getting exactly what I want, though.

I put my hands on my knees and force them down to stop my legs. But unless I hold my hands down the entire time, I'm not going to be able to hold still. Just as Beckett reenters the room, I decide to just curl my legs underneath me.

If I'm still shaking or showing any nervous energy, he doesn't seem to notice as he pours us each a glass of red wine. He hands me one, barely looking at me, and then takes a seat across from me.

We take long sips before finally staring at each other.

I'm silent. I've pushed, and now it's time for him to

open up, to tell me his secrets. And soon—he'll learn mine.

"About two years before I met Odette, I fell in love for the first time."

My eyebrows shoot up before realizing a neutral reaction is probably more helpful than a shocked one to get Beckett to talk. Quickly, I tone down my reaction and take a small sip of my drink, not interrupting him. I'll give him all the time in the world to tell his story.

"Her name was Jennifer. She was from Seattle. She ran a boat club, and that's how we met. I rented a boat for an afternoon. As soon as I saw her, I knew she was the one for me. She was the most beautiful woman I had ever met— long auburn hair, fit body, striking green eyes.

"But it was her personality that got me—bigger than life. Her laugh was infectious, her smile entrancing. Right away, I could tell she was the most caring woman I'd ever met." Beckett's face brightens as he talks about Jennifer, about this mystery woman he supposedly loved before he met Odette.

I can't help but skip ahead and assume that the only way he lost a love like her is if she died and he blames himself. I brace myself to hear about his heart being broken and the tragic story about to unfold.

"She was the one. She was my one. But my life was complicated. I'd done terrible things, killed people. Not everyone is strong enough to handle hearing that. Not everyone would accept my family with open arms. Not everyone would care less about my past, just about the man I have become.

"But Jennifer...she did. She was able to put everything aside. Not only that, but my sister-in-law, Kai, even started training her on how to use a gun and fight. She got quite good at it in the end."

Beckett sighs.

I take another drink, waiting for the bomb to drop and my heart to break for him.

"Jennifer fit in completely. She loved all my nieces and nephews. She loved being out on the water. She loved me..."

Beckett looks away at the wall.

Here it comes.

"And then one night, Enzo came to me. Some money was missing after some of our men had disobeyed Kai's orders. They said it was just a mistake, but Enzo didn't think so. He suspected Jennifer, saying something just didn't add up."

Beckett shakes his head. "I told Enzo he was crazy. I loved Jennifer, and I was going to marry her. I said he needed to accept her or get out of my life."

He swallows hard. I'm gripping onto my glass so tight I think it might break.

"And then the worst happened—Enzo's kids went missing. We'd had scares before, but never like this. They just vanished. Enzo immediately accused Jennifer. I defended her. I would have defended her to the death."

Beckett downs the rest of his drink, liquid courage to continue. "I took Jennifer, and we left to elope. I was completely blind. I did anything she said. I let love blind me. I did whatever she said, not knowing I was helping her conceal my niece and nephew. I didn't realize I was helping her blackmail my family for millions of dollars."

He's silent for a moment, but he's not done talking. He needs to finish.

"Did you eventually figure it out?"

"Yes, but it was too late. The damage had been done. The kids are traumatized by the experience. Enzo and Kai will never look at me the same. They'll never trust me; I don't even trust myself. I'm a monster for believing a woman I barely knew over my own flesh and blood. I should have believed my brother."

"You're not a monster, Beckett. She was. You figured out the truth, and then you fixed it."

"That's just it—I didn't fix it. Enzo and I never reconciled. We never talked about the situation. I continued to work for Kai as penance. When I met Odette, I found a way out. At least, that's what I thought.

"I thought the lesson I should learn was to not bring the women in my life into my world. So when I fell for Odette, I swore to never tell her the truth. I'd never work for my brother and sister-in-law again. I'd start over, and my punishment would be a life without my family."

He looks at me with a crooked grin and disgust in his eyes. "My judgment sucks, doesn't it? I keep choosing the wrong women. I keep letting people I love get hurt. I keep learning the wrong lessons. The lesson was that I can't let love be my guide. Love isn't what makes a couple work. It's not real. It's not how I should decide if I'm with a woman or not. And it's definitely not how I should decide if I spend forever with them or not."

"I couldn't agree with you more. Love isn't worth it. You should choose with your brain, not with your heart. The person who is loyal, honest, and fits you best on paper— that's how partners should be chosen."

I return Beckett's intense stare, seeing each other clearly for the first time. It doesn't matter who either of us loves. Love isn't enough, not for people like us. We need a partner. We need someone ready to take on this world. We need someone who will stand by our side as we take bullets and have our families' lives threatened.

"So who do you choose? Odette?" I ask.

For once, I'm not sure what his answer is going to be.

ODETTE

I STARE at my phone as I sit in my office. I reach for it but quickly pull my hand back into my lap—repeat times infinity. That's how I've spent my afternoon—debating whether or not I should call Ryker.

He didn't leave his number, but I had Gage get it for me. I'm sure that led the guys to a lot of questions, but I'll deal with them later. They're mostly harmless, even though I don't know whose side they are truly on. It doesn't matter. Once the war starts, even they won't be able to stop it.

Then why am I sitting here in my father's office contemplating whether or not I should be calling Ryker when I should be planning a war?

That fucking kiss.

What did the guy put into it? It wasn't tantalizing. He didn't use his tongue. It wasn't an exceptionally good kiss. It wasn't even about the kiss. When we touched, something happened. I can't explain it, but I want to understand what the hell that was.

I pick up the phone and dial Ryker's number before I change my mind again for the millionth time.

I tap my heel incessantly on the floor while I wait to see if he'll answer or not.

"Hello, Odette. I thought you'd at least wait twenty-four hours before you called me. Apparently, I made quite the impression on you," Ryker says.

I roll my eyes and consider hanging up. This was a mistake.

But I push through. More than just our connection, I need to know what his motivations are. Our interaction earlier wasn't just an accident. I don't believe in coincidences.

"What do you really want, Ryker? What was that yesterday?"

"I like it when you say my name."

I make fake gagging sounds. I hate romance. It's not real. It doesn't exist.

Beckett is a nice guy, but he was always a target. I never intended to stay married to him long-term. My plan was always to use and lose him. My father needed an heir, and I needed retribution against Enzo Black and his family.

I set everything in motion, everything that would be needed for the Retribution Kings to go to war against Enzo Black. And everything was going perfectly until Beckett fell in love with that tramp, and my plan went to hell.

So I returned from the dead to ensure my mission will be completed. Beckett was my key to doing that. Beckett and Enzo were fighting. I'd been watching them for a while, and it became clear Beckett is the key to beating Enzo. But what happened with Enzo is why I don't believe in love. I'll never believe in love and romance and happily ever afters.

Love has nothing to do with why I'm calling Ryker. I'm just making sure he's not going to ruin the plan I've been working on for years.

"Why did you plan that run-in? Why stop the elevator? What did you hope to gain?"

"Not just a pretty face. Yes, I stopped the elevator."

"Why?"

"Your bodyguards wanted me to ask you questions to find out what you're up to."

I assume he means Lennox, Gage, and Hayes, who have all been keeping close to me ever since they returned.

"Then why didn't you ask me any questions?"

"I don't take orders from them. I owed them a favor, so I met with you. But that's all I'm going to do for them. Any other questions?"

I frown. That's it? Is he not going to try and pressure me for more? He's not going to ask me what my plan is?

"Nope, just one request of my own—have dinner with me tonight," I say.

There's a pause. "Why?"

"Maybe you'd like to come work for me."

"I don't work for anyone but myself."

"Then come because I need someone to bicker with, and I think you could blow off some steam as well before the final game ends you."

"Oh, I'm going to win that game."

"Sure, you are. But in case you don't, let me buy you dinner before you die."

"Jeez, you really know how to convince a man. The answer is no."

I huff. "Fine, what do you want from me to have dinner with me?"

There's a pause.

"And I'm not sucking your dick or anything degrading," I add.

He chuckles.

"I'm not sure yet, but when I do, I'll let you know. I'll meet you at Alinea at seven-thirty."

"Wait, what do you mean you'll let me know? That's not how negotiations work. You tell me now or—"

He ends the call.

"Bastard."

He knows I'll show up; I'm too curious. But fuck him for playing games.

RYKER

I'M SITTING at a private table at Alinea at seven-thirty sharp. I doubt she will show, and if she does, it will be late. She won't give me the satisfaction of her showing up on time. I order a drink and prepare myself for a long wait.

I consider if my decision to not let the others listen in was correct or not. But I've been going with my gut as far as Odette Monroe is concerned, and so far, I've gotten further with her than the others. So I stand by my decision.

Odette would know if others were listening and I was communicating with them. She's smarter than any of us give her credit for. I just wish I could figure her out. There's still a lot of mystery around her, and all the others are too blinded by their hatred of her to actually get to know her.

"Your whiskey, sir. Is there anything else I can get you?" my waiter asks as he sets my drink down.

"No, thank you. The drink will do until Odette arrives."

He leaves, and no sooner have I taken a sip of my drink is Odette standing in front of me.

I blink rapidly, surprised to see her here so early. So much so that I choke on my drink as I stare up at her slinky red dress, striking and fierce.

She grins at my reaction.

"I'm pleased you can tell time correctly," I say.

Her smile drops as she pulls out her chair and takes a seat across from me at the white table-clothed table. "I can tell time just fine, and I'm punctual. It's just good manners not to waste someone's time. You didn't even pull out my chair for me or wait to order your drink until I arrived, so apparently, I'm the only one with manners."

I smirk at her. This creature is so fascinating to me. She's strong and independent, and her sassy mouth is beyond entertaining. I could argue with her for hours, but that's not why I'm here. I'm here to get her to spill her secrets without revealing that's actually my only goal.

"What can I get you to drink?" the waiter asks as he returns.

"I'll have what he's having," Odette says.

The waiter nods.

"So you're a whiskey girl? I took you as a white wine girl."

She rolls her eyes. "So cliche. I'm more than I appear."

"That's what fascinates me about you."

"So you're fascinated by me?" She grins and bats her eyelashes at me. *Why wouldn't every man be fascinated with her?*

"In the same way that I'm fascinated about how airplanes stay in the air. I'm not sure I'd take it as a compliment."

The waiter returns with her drink. She immediately grabs the glass, realizing she's going to need plenty of alcohol to put up with me. But it's an act. She likes bickering with me just as much as I enjoy it with her. If she didn't, she wouldn't be here.

"I didn't expect your manners to be very good after you hung up on me without answering my question," she says.

"It's killing you, isn't it? Not knowing what favor I'm going to ask of you in return for me showing up tonight," I reply.

She runs her hand over the rim of her drink. "I hate giving up control, so yes, it's bothering me. If you want me to stay, you'll tell me what favor I owe you."

"I'm not worried about you leaving. It was you who called for this dinner. It seems you are the one fascinated with me, so I think I'll hold onto the favor for a bit longer."

"One—I wanted this dinner so I could find out more about why you trapped us together in an elevator. Two—I'm fascinated with you in the same way that you are fascinated with you. And three—you can hold onto the favor you want me to do all you want; it doesn't mean I'll do it."

"You will," I tease.

She gives me a sly look. "If you're so confident, you don't know me very well."

"Or maybe I know you too well."

The waiter returns, and we inform him we're ready to begin the night's tasting menu.

"So what questions did my dear bodyguards want you to ask me?"

"The usual. Just trying to find out all your secrets so they can blackmail you. Same reason you invited me here tonight—find out dirt on me to use. Just because you are the wife of a mob boss instead of the leader yourself doesn't mean you aren't just as conniving and savage as the rest of us."

"Glad you would put the two of us on equal footing.

Most men don't see me as anything more than a trophy wife."

"Again, I think I know you pretty well."

"Because you spent twenty minutes trapped in an elevator with me or because you had me surveilled?"

"Does it matter?"

"Yes," she snaps.

"I guess you'll have to keep wondering. I won't divulge all my secrets."

She shifts her weight in her seat, and as a consequence, her foot bumps against my knee underneath the table.

I raise a brow. "You trying to give me a massage?"

She frowns. "You're a disgusting man. I'm a married woman. And you still need to apologize for that vile kiss."

"You didn't seem to mind. You didn't pull away. You didn't push me or chastise me in the moment."

"I didn't give you permission to kiss me either."

"Fair enough. I do apologize."

Her eyes widen when I apologize. "You apologize just like that?"

"I always apologize when I'm wrong. Although, based on my knowledge of you, it doesn't appear that you are happily married. It seems more like a business arrangement than a love match."

"My marriage is none of your concern."

"It is actually, seeing as I'm on a date with a married woman. I should know what I'm getting myself into. Is your husband going to hunt me down for merely having dinner with you?"

"Don't worry about that. If I want you dead, I'll be the one doing the killing."

I grin, flashing her my dimples. "I have no doubt of that."

The waiter brings out several dishes, and we both take a moment to enjoy our food before returning to interrogating one another.

"So what should we argue about now?" Odette grins at me. She enjoys arguing with me as much as I enjoy arguing with her.

"Maybe we should focus on what we have in common."

"We have things in common?"

"I think a great deal," I say.

She scoffs. "Do tell."

"We are both incredibly good-looking."

She blushes.

"We are both intelligent, witty, and both enjoy good food and a glass of whiskey," I continue.

"That's true. We're also incredibly ambitious, great leaders, and likable," she says.

"I don't find either of us very likable. But otherwise, I would agree."

She laughs. "Fine, we're very unlikable, but only because we know what we want and have high expectations of others."

We finish the last of our food, and the waiter clears our table. We both decline the dessert courses.

Looking across the table, I can see her practically bouncing in her seat with nerves. I tilt my head, smirking at her.

"You can't stand not to know, can you?" I ask.

"Know what?" she bats her eyes at me in fake confusion.

"You want to know what you owe for the enjoyment of having me at your dinner," I say.

She pulls out her purse. "I have more than enough money to pay."

I chuckle. "The task is simple."

"I'm not going to take off my underwear in public or flirt with the waiter if you're going to dare me to do something stupid like that."

"I would never insult you by asking you to do something stupid."

"Then what are you asking?"

"Simple. All I want is for you to tell me something no one else knows," I say.

She blinks at me. "That's so vague. I could answer that with practically anything, and you wouldn't know if I was telling the truth or not."

I nod. "I know you well; you won't lie to me. I know you will answer because everyone has at least one secret they want to tell. Share something real, not something small and shallow. Share something you're dying to share, something deep in your soul that needs to come out."

She stares at me for a long while. "You just want to know what scheme I'm plotting. You want to know about Beckett and Rialta and all the others."

"No, actually. I don't care what you share; just share a part of your soul so I may better know and understand you. That's all I've ever wanted as far as you're concerned," I say.

"And you'll tell me a secret in return?"

I chuckle. "If I feel like it. But since your secret is payment for me being here tonight, I'll have to see if your secret is worthy of one of my own."

She stills for a moment, and I think I was wrong. She's not going to divulge anything.

"I'll tell you a secret, but not here."

She stands, and I follow.

"You're going to owe me an awfully big secret if I'm to follow you to a second location," I say.

"I know, but you'll come."

"How do you know that?"

"For the same reason you knew I'd tell you a secret."

"Which is?" I ask.

"Fascination."

21

ODETTE

R YKER WALKS me out of the restaurant, and for once, I don't feel completely in control. Not because he's taken control from me, but because I feel myself losing it. I want to give up a bit of control when I'm with him.

Fuck, what am I doing?

We make it outside when I say, "You can follow me in your car."

"Or I can ride with you," he says back.

I swallow hard. "Or you can ride with me."

We walk to my Maserati, and Ryker slides into the passenger seat while I slide behind the wheel. I start the car and begin backing out of my parking spot.

"Odette!" Ryker yells and I slam on my brakes.

I look in my rearview mirror and see that I about backed into a couple walking into the restaurant. The woman flashes me a dirty look, and the man flips me off.

"Maybe I should drive," Ryker says.

I run my hands through my hair and shake the nervous energy off. I tilt my head side to side and roll my shoulders back. I look Ryker dead in the eyes. "No, I've got this."

He nods, his eyes skimming over me before he buckles his seatbelt and lets me take control.

Most men would have insisted on driving after that little blunder, but not Ryker. He still trusts me. That or his desire to get answers far outweighs his will to live.

I make it out onto the road and start driving through downtown streets. We aren't going far. We just need to go somewhere the three idiots won't have already set up cameras to record us, somewhere where we can truly be alone.

Ryker doesn't ask any questions. He also doesn't show any signs of nervousness or distress as I drive through the city streets. He seems completely at ease next to me.

After driving for twenty minutes, I pull the car into the valet of my favorite hotel chain.

Ryker's eyes dart up at the tower above us and then looks at me. "If I knew we were getting a hotel room, I wouldn't have argued about coming."

I shake my head. "Just because I brought you to a hotel doesn't mean you're going to score."

"It doesn't mean I'm not going to either." He winks at me.

I glare back.

He shrugs. "It doesn't matter where you take me. I can make you want me in a dark alleyway next to a dumpster if I want."

"So full of yourself." The valet opens my door and helps me out.

"Do you have any bags I can take for you?" the valet asks.

"No," I reply.

Then Ryker is by my side. He holds out his arm, waiting for me to decide if I want to take it or not.

I hesitate for just a second before I hook my arm through his, and we walk inside. Ryker leads me to the front desk.

"Hello, Mrs. Monroe. Your usual?" the woman behind the front desk asks when she sees me.

I nod.

Ryker studies me closely out of the corner of his eye as she slides a key to me.

"Enjoy your stay," the receptionist says.

And then we are in the elevators riding up to the top floor.

"You take men who aren't your husband to this hotel often?" Ryker asks.

I grin. "You'll never know."

He narrows his eyes. "I'm going to take that as a no."

"Take it however you want; it doesn't make it true."

The doors open, and we begin walking down the hallway to my suite as I continue holding onto Ryker's arm. Once inside, I let go of his arm, and he takes a minute to survey the spacious room.

"Still think you have enough money to compete with me?" I ask teasingly.

He smirks. "I own real estate properties that are more expensive than this entire hotel. Yes, I can compete with you on money, but I'm not going to."

I start walking toward the living room. I want to talk. I need someone to talk to, someone to hear my story. Someone who has very little to no reason to hate me.

"Do you think I'm a monster?" I ask before I sit down on the couch. There are plenty of stories to tell him, but the one I need to share the most depends on his answer to this question.

He stares out the floor-to-ceiling windows a second while he debates his answer.

"You could say we are all monsters."

I hold my breath, waiting for him to continue.

"But I prefer to think of us all as humans doing our best to survive in a world where many won't. We all do what it takes to survive as long as we can. We all do plenty of immoral things. We all steal, threaten, and murder. Only true monsters take without need. They hurt others out of pure enjoyment. They murder not out of protection or need but just because they like to see the light leave people's eyes."

I swallow hard, not sure where he considers me on this scale.

He stares me down as if reading my soul.

"You, Odette, are not a monster. Everything you do is for survival."

"And revenge," I add.

I wait for him to say that makes me a monster. I've forced Beckett to fuck me almost every night we were together, even though he hates it. That is the very definition of a monster, according to Ryker, and he'd be right.

"Do you think that makes you a monster? Seeking revenge on those who have hurt you?"

"Yes. I enjoy the pain and suffering of those who have hurt me," I say.

He smiles. "You aren't a monster."

"How do you figure?"

"A monster wouldn't admit they are a monster and feel guilt about it. You do."

"How do you know?" I ask.

"I can see it in your eyes. You're disappointed by what you did, ashamed even. We are all human. We all do things we shouldn't; that doesn't make you a monster."

I take a seat, and Ryker mirrors me, sitting on the couch opposite me. Everything he just said could have been because he wants me to open up to him. He could have an ulterior motive.

But just like he senses things about me, I sense things about him. And I need to talk to someone. Everyone who knows about my past is dead—my father and my brother. I'm all alone in this world.

"I was kidnapped, assaulted, and raped," I say.

"That's common knowledge. Although, I'm so sorry for what happened to you," he says quietly.

I shake my head. "What I shared was a lie. Enzo didn't kidnap me—this time. But he has before."

Ryker's eyes widen ever so slightly, but he doesn't react otherwise.

"When I was eighteen, Vincent Corsi's men took me from my home. They didn't hurt me, didn't touch me, really. They held me in a clean hotel room. They fed me, let me watch TV. It was all very civil. I just thought they were ransoming my father or upset with something he did. I wasn't afraid. I knew my father and brother would come for me. They'd pay whatever price Corsi demanded."

I close my eyes, trying to remain emotionless as I speak, but it's near impossible when the images flood my brain again. The trauma lives in every fiber of my body. I can pretend the memories don't exist, but they are always there, just hovering below the surface, ready to overwhelm me at any time.

"My father never came, neither did my brother. Someone else far more sinister did," I continue.

I keep my eyes closed as I speak. I keep the pain in, the tears in.

I don't care about Ryker's reaction. I don't care if he believes me or not. I just need to tell someone. I need to remember why I'm doing this.

"Enzo Black was the one who showed up. He paid for me like he was buying a horse. And for the first time, I knew what it felt like to be terrified. He tied my arms, my legs, and he gagged me. He tossed me in his trunk like a piece of garbage, not a human.

"For hours, we drove, and I could barely breathe stuffed in that trunk. He didn't care. He didn't check on me. He didn't feed me. Nothing."

I swallow down the lump in my throat as I get to the next part, the worst part, the part I wish I could forget.

"Enzo carried me from the car. I barely had any energy to fight. And even if I could, my father never taught me how to get out bindings like that. I was helpless.

"Inside, things got worse. He removed my bindings only to tie me to a bed. I heard Enzo and his father talking. I was a daughter of a crime boss. Enzo wanted to sell me as quickly as possible. He didn't want to start a war, but his father wasn't afraid of a fight. He wasn't afraid of the Retribution Kings. He wanted to send a message that he was far more powerful than my father."

The tears slip, but I don't open my eyes. I let the water streak down my cheek as I carry on.

"I was there for five days, but it might as well have been five years. I was assaulted and raped in every way imaginable. I thought it would never end. I thought I would be there forever. Then one day, I was dropped back off in front of my father's doorstep.

"Naked.

"Beaten.

"Abused."

I clear my throat.

"I woke up before my father did. I paid for a hotel room, and I stayed there until I healed. I didn't tell my father what happened, at least not until a few years later. That's when a plan started to form."

I open my eyes. "I want to destroy them all. I need to destroy them all. Everyone involved I need revenge against. Beckett is the weak link. He didn't hurt me directly, but he's Enzo's brother. He works for him, has done horrible things for him. He was my way in, and I don't feel guilty about punishing Beckett and everyone in Enzo's family for Enzo and his father's crimes."

Finally, I look at Ryker. There are tears in his eyes. His nostrils are flared. His face is a deep red. His hands are fisted at his side, and his knees bounce anxiously.

"Don't pity me. I don't want or need your pity," I spit.

He opens his mouth and then closes it. Over and over, he does this before I see tears streaming down his own face.

I stand up abruptly, not able to face his sorrow. "I told you not to pity me."

"I don't pity you. I'm heartbroken at what you went through. But I'm also so incredibly awestruck by how brave and strong you are, how much of a fighter you are."

I turn and face him. He doesn't retreat even though we're standing so close that a strong wind could push us into each other.

"I don't need you to be in awe of me. I'm just a human

who has been hurt and betrayed, and I want revenge. It's the only way to squash the nightmares."

He grins down at me in his sexy way. "You should get the revenge you seek. But are you sure that revenge is the only way to get rid of the nightmares?"

The next thing I know, he leans in and kisses me. It's a soft and tender kiss at first, giving me plenty of room to pull away. But when I don't, he grabs the back of my neck and kisses me hungrily.

And as soon as our tongues touch, I never want him to stop.

22

RYKER

I'VE NEVER BEEN SO ATTRACTED to someone in my life. Her strength, her courage, her beauty—everything about her I want.

She's like me in a lot of ways. We're both leaders that do what we have to in order to survive. We don't share our plans with many others. And although she didn't share her exact plan when it came to Ri, she shared an awful lot.

Odette shared her darkest secret, a hidden piece of her soul. It's the part that defines her, the part that explains everything.

Everyone sees her as this evil adversary who wants to take them down for the sake of hurting them, for power and money and control.

In reality, she's a woman who's been hurt in the worst possible way seeking retribution for what happened to her. And I can relate to that.

Ri doesn't deserve to die for what happened to Odette, though. Enzo deserves to pay for what he and his father did; so does Corsi. And Beckett...I'm not sure what his role is exactly yet in all of this, but if he knew and did nothing, then he deserves to pay as well.

I kiss Odette with everything I have, assuming she's going to stop me at any moment. She doesn't want my pity, so kissing her is the only way I can think of to show her how incredible I think she is.

Fuck, she tastes amazing.

Her body leans into mine, and I about lose it. I want to rip her dress off. I want to fuck her against the window and claim her as mine.

But she's not mine...

I gently pull away, stopping the kiss and everything else before this goes too far.

"I'm sorry," I say.

Her grin is so wide I must be hallucinating. "You have nothing to be sorry for; that kiss was incredible."

"It was, wasn't it?" I smirk. "I'm not sorry about the kiss, even if you are a married woman. I'm sorry about my intentions. I am here to try and find a way to protect Ri, but there's something more here. Something has shifted between us. I still want to protect Ri, she's my friend, but I also understand everything about you."

Odette stiffens at the mention of Ri, so I continue.

"Thank you for sharing your story with me. I'll protect it with everything I have. I don't want to be your enemy anymore; I want to be honest with you."

"I already knew that's why you approached me. Rialta will be safe as long as the others don't interfere with my plan for revenge."

I nod. "Thank you."

We stand awkwardly in front of each other as the tension grows.

"I should go," I say.

"Or you should kiss me again." There's a twinkle in her eyes, a wanting only I can fulfill.

"You belong to Beckett, and I've already touched someone who belonged to him once. I'm not sure I have the strength to do it again."

"I don't belong to Beckett. He belongs to me. But if it helps, I won't touch him again," she says.

I bite the back of my knuckles as she pushes out her chest and licks her bottom lip.

God, do I want her. I want her so fucking badly. But then what? We can't date. We can't even fuck regularly. I still want to protect Ri. And I can't lead my men to war, but...

"Fuck me, Ryker. I'm not asking you to marry me or fight in a war; just fuck me tonight."

I growl and then attack her.

"Tonight, you're mine, Odette," I bark.

I kiss her just as she's about to respond, catching her mouth open. Our teeth clash together in an aggressive kiss. Our bodies collide, and my hand goes to her ass, yanking her to me. My other hand grabs her neck, tilting her head to deepen the kiss.

Her hands are clutched tightly around my neck as if she's afraid I'm going to break the kiss again and run out the door. She needs this as much as I do. She needs a connection to someone who actually wants her, not stuck in a marriage for revenge.

I don't know what this is. *Just one night? The start of something more? The beginning of a friendship or alliance? Or a one-time reprieve before we fight on opposite sides of a war?* Whatever this is, I'm going to enjoy it. And I'm damn sure going to make sure she enjoys it too.

We're on the top floor of a high-rise building, but I

need everyone to know that tonight this fearless and hot as fuck woman is mine. I'm the one making her scream, making her come.

I grab her ass with both hands, and she gladly wraps her legs around my waist as I walk us back toward the floor-to-ceiling windows. The lights are on, and it's getting dark outside. If anyone looks in our direction, they will be able to see everything.

I press her back against the wall as I devour her mouth. I'm not gentle. Maybe I should be, but I'm trusting my instincts here unless she tells me otherwise. My gut says to show her how much I want her.

With the window helping to support her back, I move a free hand from her ass to beneath her dress. I don't waste any time inching my hand up her thigh until I feel the wetness between her legs.

"No panties, naughty girl."

She whimpers against my lips, and her hips shift, begging for me to touch her aching clit.

But I'm a cruel man, and I want to hear her beg first. Quickly, I remove my hand.

She pulls back from the kiss, and I realize I just made a huge mistake. She's about to tell me to take a hike since I didn't do things her way. Instead, she grabs my chin and glares at me.

"I don't like to be toyed with," she says.

I smirk and run a finger down her neck to the top of her cleavage. "You're going to have to learn to be patient if you want me to fuck you. I won't rush the time I have with you."

"Fine, but I can tease too."

"I look forward to it," I reply.

I lean in for a kiss, but at the last second, she turns her

head. My kiss lands on her cheek instead of her lips.

I growl my response. This woman is either going to be the best or worst thing for me; I just can't figure out which. I wish I would know the answer before I fuck her and lose myself to her completely.

I lick down her cheek to her neck as her hand creeps down the front of my chest, lower and lower, until she reaches the top of my jeans. I fully expect her to stop and barely tease me. I try to keep my cock from getting too excited, but it's straining hard against the zipper in my jeans.

She undoes the snap, then the zipper, and I hold my breath, expecting utter denial of her touch. But then her hand dips down beneath my underwear and grazes the curve of my cock.

My head falls back as she strokes the top of my cock. It's not even the most sensitive part, but I feel like I'm about to explode into a million pieces.

I groan as she roughly pulls me out of my boxer briefs and wraps her entire hand around my cock. My eyes are closed as she pumps me, making me almost lose my goddamned mind.

And then I feel wetness being spread over my cock, warming me and making every touch that much more incredible.

I open my eyes, realizing what she's doing. She's using my cock as her personal dildo, rubbing it against her clit since I wouldn't give her what she wanted.

I grab her wrist, stopping her. "You play dirty."

She bites down on her lip, trying to hide a smile.

I lick over her lips until she lets my tongue in, swirling around to take control once again. I reach behind her and find the zipper on her dress. Quickly, I pull it down, tracing my fingers down her back as she trembles in my arms.

"Why do your fingers on my spine alone feel so good?" she wonders out loud.

"The same reason everything else does. You and I share a spark, a rare connection I thought wasn't real. Plus, I'm a damn good lover, baby."

She rolls her eyes and pinches my butt. "I've yet to see how good of a lover you are since you won't actually fuck me."

I shake my head. "So impatient."

And then I yank her dress down her body until it's bunching at her waist.

"No bra either." My eyes lock in on her gorgeous breasts.

Her eyes stare down at me as her chest heaves, and her breathing slows.

I lick my lips in a slow circle—the same way I plan on encircling her nipples.

She purses her lips, trying to remain in control.

And then, I slowly dip my head toward the closest nipple. Her hand grabs the back of my head, and she pushes me down until her nipple grazes my lips.

I laugh before licking around her pink point until she's panting. Then I make the same motion to the other nipple.

She arches her back into the window as she holds my head firmly against her breast.

"Do you want me to touch you?" I mutter in between licks.

"Yes."

"Then you have to beg."

"I don't beg."

I chuckle. "You will."

I press my cock between her legs, letting her clit feel the pressure of me there, but not more. I don't move, just hold firmly against her. And then I devour her neck, her breasts, her lips—everything but what she actually wants.

Her breath speeds, and she drenches me in wetness. I'm fucking aching to be inside her, to touch her, to give us both the satisfaction. But it's up to her. I can be patient. I can hold out until she begs. At least I think I can, but each second that goes by is harder and harder.

I can't take it any longer. I—

"Please," she begs.

One word.

One syllable.

But it's enough.

"Thank fuck," I groan.

I set her down and yank her dress off until she's completely bare in front of me.

"So fucking incredible," I gasp.

She rakes her teeth over her bottom lip as I spin her around so the entire world can see what I get tonight. This woman is mine.

My hand sneaks around the front of her body and finally gives her what she's been begging for—I stroke her clit.

Her knees give out as I stroke her. "Is it too much?" I tease.

"Don't you dare stop!"

I chuckle low and deep as I shift behind her, my cock pressing against her ass. My other hand fumbles with a condom from the pocket of my jeans. I slip it on as she moans loudly for me; I'm barely able to control myself.

"If you keep moaning like that, I'm going to come

before I'm even inside you."

"Don't you dare! I need you," she moans.

That's all it takes for me to lose any resemblance of control. I grab her hips, and then my cock is inside her in one long stroke.

Her face and chest press against the window as my fingers continue to work her swollen bud. She rocks against me, meeting every thrust, her moans growing louder and completely unfiltered. She doesn't care if the entire hotel can hear her. It drives me to make it even better for her, to see what other sounds I can pull for her.

This woman deserves the best damn sex a man can give her. And I plan on giving her just that.

I pump into her faster as my fingers run circles over her clit. Her nipples are pressed hard against the windowpane, as is her cheek.

My lips brush over her earlobe, and then I kiss down her neck, eliciting more moans vibrating from her throat.

"How close are you, baby?" I moan, knowing I'm not going to be able to hold on much longer.

"Ryker!" she screams as she begins to fall apart around me.

I come right along with her, losing complete control.

She falls back into me, and I barely have the strength to catch her and keep myself upright. I carry her back to the couch behind us, where I collapse with her on top of me and my arms around her.

She doesn't struggle to get away. She lets me hold her, but I don't know how long this will last. I don't know what our future holds. I doubt we'll be together despite how I feel when I'm around her.

I do know one thing, though. I'm going to do everything I can to ensure she lets me fuck her again.

"SO, WHO DO YOU CHOOSE? ODETTE?" I ask.

He doesn't answer me. He opens his mouth and then closes it like he can't bring himself to answer. That is an answer in of itself.

If he loved her like he's said in the past, if he would move heaven and earth for her, he'd choose her. If it's always been her, as he claims, this would be an easy proclamation.

Beckett takes a deep breath, and I mirror him. Our breaths start slow as we try to remain calm. With each passing second, our breaths quicken. Faster and faster until our hyperventilating is the only thing I can feel. We're out of control. Whatever we do next, it won't be something we planned. It won't be something we think all the way through.

It will be reckless, stupid, and carnal. We won't be using logic. Our brains are turned off—something that should never happen, especially now that I know the truth.

I can't be reckless.

I can't be selfish.

I can't...

And yet, I'm about to do or say something very stupid.

No.

It's smart.

Tactical.

At least that's what I convince myself.

It's clear Beckett doesn't love Odette. I don't know his motives exactly for why he stays with her, and it doesn't really matter. But I wonder...does he love me?

"You told me you loved me once. I'm sure you've said the same to Odette many times." My words come out gentler and calmer than I thought they would.

"How could you?" I snap.

Beckett tilts his head, looking at me with deep pain in his eyes.

"How dare you play with our emotions like that! How dare you lie to us!" My voice cracks as I toss my wine glass on the floor, and it shatters into a million tiny shards.

I stand up.

Beckett is on his feet instantly. He's not going to cower. He's not going to just take it. He's not going to just let me attack him.

"I did what I had to to get what I wanted. I'm a monster. It's not my fault if you didn't see that."

"Bastard."

His nostrils flare wide as he clenches his jaw. He's so close to breaking, to admitting the absolute truth. *But am I ready to hear it?*

"Fuck you, Hero!"

"I'm not your hero. You were stupid enough to think that. I'm your villain, the man who will take everything from you."

"You're right, you are my villain, and I'm tired of waiting to figure out what your next move is. You want to win the game? You want to choose my husband, control my father's empire? Then take it." I grab the hem of my shirt and lift it over my head, and I'm naked again in front of him.

His eyes bulge, and I can hear his teeth grinding together as he tries to hold it together.

"Take it! Take what you want from me! That's all I'm good for anyway—a hole you can fuck! A pawn in your game you can move and sacrifice and take whatever you want from. So take from me! Win the fucking game! End this!"

Beckett takes a step forward; I don't move.

"Ri," he says, his voice soft and breaking.

He keeps walking closer until he's standing inches in front of me.

What is he going to do? Kiss me? Fuck me? Threaten me? Tell me the truth?

He does none of those things. He bends down and picks up the shirt lying on the floor.

"Please," he says, not even looking at me as he shoves the shirt into my chest.

I grab his hand. "Look at me, you coward!"

His eyes drift in my direction, and I see unending pain, but I also see something else...*lust.*

That one look, and I know I'm going to do the wrong thing, the reckless thing, the regrettable thing. But it's my last chance to be selfish. And I can at least learn one thing from my impulsive actions...

I grab his cheeks, and I pull him into a hard kiss. It's a brass kiss, a kiss of pure desperation and need and...

He kisses me back—just as desperate, full of just as much need.

I can't breathe as the kiss consumes everything inside me. I forget how to take in air, but I'd gladly die in this kiss.

"Breathe, Ri," he whispers in between kisses.

I can't. If I take a second to breathe, it's a moment for him to come to his senses and put an end to this.

So as he pulls his lips off mine, I attack with mine, gasping into his lips as my body falls against his. I grab his hips, pressing them hard against mine, not letting him roll away.

Our tongues tangle, and Beckett grabs one of my thighs, hiking it up against his leg.

"I want this, Fighter. I want you," he says.

I don't know if it's the alcohol talking or the lust or what, but he won't back out now. Not an earthquake or a bomb dropping; nothing will stop us. That fact doesn't slow me down, though. I've spent too long without this man touching me, kissing me, fucking me. All because I thought he loved another woman. All because I thought he betrayed me.

I grab the collar of his shirt and rip, pulling it aggressively down in half and scraping my nails along his bare chest over the tattoo that claims his loyalty to the Retribution Kings. I trace the crown of the tattoo that is meaningless. He can mark his body all he wants, but no one knows where his true loyalty lies. I don't know. Odette doesn't know. His family doesn't know. His friends don't know.

He captures my hand in his and kisses the palm. I can feel the kiss through my entire body.

I grab his jeans and undo them just enough to yank

them down his body until he's as bare as me. When our naked skin touches, it's all over.

Our animal instincts take over. Our minds cease to exist. Our bodies collide in a tangle of arms and legs as we fall to the floor together.

The shards from my wine glass stick into our backs, but the pain won't stop us—nothing will.

I straddle Beckett as I kiss him, starting from his lips, down his neck, and over his stomach until I reach his cock. Usually, I'd take him slowly, tease him and get us turned on. We're already both so turned on that none of that is necessary. And while nothing will stop us, plenty of things could try, and I'm not taking that chance.

I take all of him in my mouth, swirling my tongue around his tip as he lightly thrusts into my mouth, hitting the back of my throat. I love how he tastes in my mouth as I lick up and down the length of him, savoring every drop of him, feeling every ridge of his veins. I indulge in every moan he makes as I suck him.

As soon as I popped the head of his cock out from my lips, he's grabbed my hip and is pulling me up his body. He doesn't stop until my hips hover over his chin.

I won't deny myself any longer. I let my hips sink down on top of his face as his tongue slides up and down my slit. My wetness intensifies as he finds my clit and applies just the right amount of pressure with his tongue. His hand palms my breast, teasing my nipple.

I'm mush on top of him. My body feels like jello as he works me into a frenzy. I'm along for the ride but no longer in control. I can't move my limbs. I can barely keep myself upright as his tongue brings me closer to orgasm.

He doesn't have to say a word, not a single syllable. He

doesn't have to tell me to come. He doesn't have to ask if I'm coming. He just knows.

Fuck, he knows everything about my body.

I love how he pays attention to me. I love how he watches for signs of what I like and don't like without asking. I love how he worships my body.

Suddenly I can't hold back my screams any longer.

I come undone on his face as his tongue dips in and out of me. I moan loudly but don't speak a syllable, afraid that if I do, the spell we're both under might be broken.

I collapse, slamming my hips down, my vagina covering his face, probably suffocating him. But he doesn't seem to care; he doesn't push me off.

I fall forward, grabbing the coffee table to keep me from collapsing completely face down.

Beckett gives me a second to regain my strength before he slides me down his body. My wetness coats his abs until I feel his hard cock at my ass.

I grab his cock, sliding it between my folds, coating him in my moisture. And then, with my eyes locked on Beckett's, I align our bodies and slide down onto his thick cock.

I groan as he fills me completely. It's more than just fulfilling a sexual need for me, but I don't let my mind go there. I focus on Beckett, on his reaction. *Is it more than just sex for him?*

He thrusts into me with everything he has. His hand grabs my hip, helping me move up and down on his cock. His eyes are glossy with lust and desire. The sounds he makes are animalistic and carnal. His actions all point to one thing.

I ride him harder, focusing more on the moment and my impending orgasm instead of Beckett's reactions.

His hand moves between my legs, rubbing on my clit as I get closer and closer to falling over the edge.

We still haven't spoken, still haven't shared any feelings. It feels more like a one-night stand than two people who know and care about each other.

As I start to get close, Beckett flips us over, pushing me beneath him and continuing his thrusts inside me. It deepens the angle and allows him better access to my body.

His eyes darken as he thrusts harder and deeper while his thumb rubs my sensitive clit. I'm about to come, but I try to hold it back, knowing that when I do, it could be all over. This is the last fucking time we are together. The last time ever.

I've thought that before, felt it. But this time is different. This time I know deep in my soul, I know in my barely functioning brain. This is the last time. There will never be another moment like this.

But Beckett is too good a lover; I couldn't hold back my orgasm if I tried. My orgasm explodes through my body, knocking me even more out of my body as I come. My head falls back, and my eyes fall closed as I just let myself feel everything happening in my body, as I get to experience him—all of him—one last time.

Beckett still hasn't spoken. I haven't either.

My eyes slowly open, and I see Beckett staring down at me with dark eyes.

No words are exchanged.

No feelings.

No mention of love.

Acceptance washes over me.

He doesn't love Odette.

And he doesn't love me. Our connection is one-sided

lust, filled with my yearning. He doesn't return the sentiment.

And almost as if to prove my point, he stands and walks away without a word, leaving me naked on the floor.

I guess he got what he wanted. A chance to win the game. A chance to get me pregnant.

I sit up slowly as a warm liquid flows down my belly. I look down and am shocked by what I see—Beckett's cum covers my stomach. He didn't come inside me. He didn't try to win the game. He just fucked me.

I stare at the door he just left through, more confused about his feelings than ever. But I am closer to making a decision, and the games are about to end.

24

BECKETT

I can't think. I have to get out of this room. I can't be in the same space as her for another second, or I'm going to crack. All I can do is get myself away from Ri, so that's exactly what I do.

I walk out of the room. I can't even tell her what I'm doing; I'm so close to the edge of spilling everything, even if it risks Ri's life. That's the opposite of what I want.

I run my hand through my hair as I pace in the empty hallway. I wish any of the guys were here; I need someone to talk to. I need someone to remind me why I can't tell her the truth. I need someone to talk some sense into me before I do something I'll regret.

I walk down the hallway and find my phone still lying on the kitchen counter where I left it. I need information. I need to know if the guys have figured out Odette's plan, or anything at all, yet.

After fucking Ri, being so close, holding her in my arm, I need some hope. I don't know how I'm going to give her up. I've known I loved her for a long time, but having her again after everything that happened, after sharing

171

everything with her, after her still clearly loving me—it's much more difficult to let her go. I'm not sure I'm strong enough this time to give her up permanently.

I dial Gage's number and wait. He answers on the third ring. "Tell me you have something. Tell me you found out anything we can use to blackmail Odette. Tell me she spilled her guts. Tell me something good."

Gage hesitates; they have nothing.

"Well...Ryker made some headway with Odette," he begins tepidly.

"Oh, thank god."

"Yea, um, the two of them are real close...um..." he stutters.

I frown. "Gage, are you trying to tell me that Ryker slept with my wife? I don't care. In fact, I'd be grateful if he's with her. Maybe she'll find someone who isn't me to sink her teeth into."

"Yes, Ryker and Odette have become a bit of a thing, although not publicly. They're keeping their relationship secret," he says.

"Great. What has he found out? Any details? Has he gotten close to figuring out how to prevent her from attacking Ri?"

"Um...I'm not sure...I guess...I'm not...it's just..."

"Jesus Christ, man, spit it out."

There's a pause, and then Hayes comes on the phone. "You need to get back here, right the hell now."

"Why?"

"They're going to attack your brother at midnight," Hayes says.

"Who is 'they?'" My chest seizes at the thought of Odette going to battle with my brother. He and his family have been through so much. They don't deserve to have to go through another war. I'm having a heart attack at the thought of anything happening to my family. Despite everything that has happened between us, they're still my family. I'll do everything I can to protect my family.

"Odette is leading the Retribution Kings. She has practically everyone on her side. And..." Hayes trails off. If he speaks, it's barely audible, more of a mumble.

"Jesus, put Lennox on," I say, fed up with both Hayes and Gage.

After a moment, Lennox begins filling in the details for me. "Ryker—he's leading his men to fight in the battle side-by-side with the Retribution Kings. He's also rounding up some of the other local crime organizations and rallying them to his side. They're trying to convince them to take down the great Enzo Black first, so they'll be strong enough to go after Corsi."

"Fuck! How could you guys let this happen?" Apparently, I didn't have to worry about the three of them being spies for Odette. I should have been worried about Ryker falling in love with the bitch. I should have seen it coming. It's what she did to me.

"You wanted us to get information any way possible. The three of us failed, so we sent in Ryker. We didn't think he'd actually fall for her schemes," Lennox says.

"Are you sure he's fallen for her? He isn't just playing her to get information?" I ask. It's the only thing left I can hope for.

"Maybe? He's not talking to us at the moment, so I don't think so."

"Fuck," I swear again.

That's when I hear her footsteps behind me on the wooden floor. I turn and look at Ri.

She's beautiful and still very naked in front of me. My

cum is still dripping off her abs. All I want to do is drag her to the closest bedroom and fuck her again and again.

I don't care about the game. I don't care about getting her pregnant. I just want her to be mine.

She stares at me, trying to read the situation.

I'm sure I look hopeless as I stand naked in front of her. There's lust in my eyes when I look at her, but nothing in hers except careful examination.

"They're currently in a meeting planning their attack. Gage says he overheard via his cameras that the go time is midnight."

I don't respond at first. I don't want Ri to know anything is wrong, but I need to tell them something.

"Tell Gage to find out everything he can, and the rest of you need to stall as long as you can." I hang up the phone. I'm not sure what I'm going to do, but I can't stay here.

"Everything okay?" Ri asks.

I laugh. "Everything is never okay."

She smiles at that. Then she says, "I'm ready for you to take me back to Chicago."

"You are?"

"Yes, I know who I'm going to choose."

She isn't going to tell me. Her one-sentence terrifies me as much as Lennox's words. I can't fight two wars at once, but I don't have a choice.

"Then let's go home," I say.

GAGE

FIND OUT EVERYTHING, he says. Like we haven't been trying to do that this whole time.

Stall, he says. I don't know how you stall a war when the woman in charge has clearly been planning this exact moment, but I'll try.

I look to Lennox and Hayes; they look as desperate as I feel. Although Beckett is rushing back to do what he can to stop this, he's not going to make it in time.

"We failed at getting information from Odette, but we're not going to fail at stalling this," I say.

The other two nod their heads. "We don't even know where Enzo Black and his family are. Even if Odette leads the Retribution Kings out of here at midnight, it doesn't mean they will be able to attack anytime soon. We just need to stall them, make it harder for them to leave," Lennox says.

I agree. "We won't fail, not this time."

"So, what's the plan?" Hayes asks, looking at me. I'm not the one who usually makes the plans, but I know why they both look to me now. I'm the only one who can hack into any computer system. I'm the one that Beckett trusts the most among us three.

"Hayes, work on Odette. Lennox work on Ryker. I'm going to put cameras on everyone I can and see if anyone talks. We need to figure out their plan. Last we knew, Enzo Black and his crew were in the Caribbean. We need to figure out how they plan on attacking and getting there. Maybe we can stall them by blowing out some tires or engines."

"I'll trade you," Hayes says to Lennox.

"Not a chance in hell. It's your turn to work Odette," Lennox responds.

I attach tiny cameras to both men. "Go."

"What are you going to do, again?" Hayes frowns, clearly annoyed that he was put on Odette.

"What I do best," I grin.

He rolls his eyes.

After a short car ride, we park outside the warehouse that is the Retribution Kings' operations center. There was once a time when we felt like we owned this building. A time when we were the top of the Retribution Kings, set to be leaders. Now I'm not sure how any of them look at us.

Betrayers?

Accomplices?

Outcasts?

Nonetheless, we walk inside like we own the place. We keep our heads up, our chests out, and our eyes downcast like everyone is beneath us.

No one speaks to us; no one tries to kick us out. I'd like to see them try.

I divert to the right, to some of the gathered gang leaders, while Lennox and Hayes continue forward to where Odette and Ryker are.

I push my way through the crowd, putting small cameras on everyone in sight and making my way toward the side alleyway where I can monitor the feeds. I won't be able to hide forever without people getting suspicious of planted cameras now that they've seen me, but I don't need long. People like to talk.

I pull out my phone and check Lennox's and Hayes's cameras first.

"Buzz off, Hayes, I don't need you pestering me right now," Odette says.

Hayes doesn't budge. "I'm under strict orders from Beckett to protect you at all costs. If there's going to be a war, I need to make sure you're safe. Beckett would hate to lose you again."

She scoffs. "I'm sure."

I flip the screen to Lennox. "What the hell are you doing, Ryker?"

Ryker brushes past him.

"What would Ri say?" Lennox tries again.

Ryker stops for just a second but thinks better of talking to Lennox and keeps walking.

Dammit.

I flip to the other leaders. "I'm not going all the way to the Caribbean to fight Enzo Black, not where he has the edge. His yachts are indestructible. It doesn't matter how many men we bring. We'd never win there," one says.

Another man responds, "We aren't going to the Caribbean. Odette and Beckett lured them here with a meeting to talk peace."

They laugh together.

Shit.

We need info now.

I head back inside toward Ryker.

"Not you too," Ryker says.

"Just tell us what happened," I plead.

"I can't."

I pat Ryker on the shoulder, planting a camera. "Then, I just hope you know what you're getting yourself into."

Quickly, I walk toward the other exit. I pull my phone back up and flip to the feed of Ryker. He walks toward Odette, telling Hayes to go fuck himself.

Hayes eventually leaves, and then it's just the two of them.

They don't touch each other. After all, everyone thinks Odette is married to Beckett. But it's obvious how they feel about each other. They like each other a lot, maybe even love each other.

Fuck.

Ryker is no longer ours. He's on her side, and I don't know how to stop this.

Ryker gets close to Odette, and I think he might lean in to kiss her or touch her at least. He doesn't, but he says in a hushed tone, "If I do this, Ri lives. No matter what."

Odette looks at him and then nods.

Maybe I was wrong. Ryker just got us the one thing Beckett asked of us—stop Odette from hurting Ri. But it's at the cost of his family. Beckett wants us to stop this war, but if we do, Ri won't be safe.

I don't know what he wants us to do now that it's gotten even more complicated.

26

RI

BECKETT IS an anxious mess as we drive back. He hasn't spoken since telling me to get dressed and hopping in the car with me. I haven't really talked either, but as we get closer to the city, my own worry grows. It'd be nice to hear from him why he's in a rush to get back.

"What happened?" I ask.

He doesn't respond.

I huff. "Really? You're not going to talk to me?"

"Who did you choose?" Beckett tosses back at me.

I frown, not ready to talk about that.

"Exactly," he huffs and keeps driving.

I don't ask any questions again, but it doesn't take long for me to get some answers.

"What, Gage?" Beckett snaps into his phone.

He listens carefully and then goes white. Beckett doesn't say anything, but I can read his face well enough.

"Did war break out?" I ask.

The look he gives me confirms it.

"Fuck," I whisper, hating it as much as he does. Even if my own family isn't involved—yet. Vincent Corsi always gets involved in war eventually, though. It's how he shows and keeps his power. It's only a matter of time until this is my problem too.

Beckett starts dialing numbers on his phone. "Pick up, pick up, pick up!"

Whoever he's calling doesn't answer.

"I need a gun," I say.

"Glove compartment."

I pop it open and find a fully loaded gun and knife. I take both.

We pull into a parking lot to the sound of gunfire.

"Holy shit," I say.

"What?" Beckett asks.

"That's one of Corsi's men. Apparently, we're already involved in this fight."

I step out of the car, and Beckett follows me.

"Beckett, what day is it?" I ask as chills creep over my skin.

"The fifteenth."

I start running.

"Ri!" Beckett yells. "Ri, slow down! You can't fight them all on your own!"

"Watch me!" I shout as I fire into the back of a man crouched down behind a car.

The parking lot is for a warehouse along Lake Michigan. Men are fighting in alleyways, from the water, and along the shoreline. Police won't be showing up to put a stop to this, as I'm sure someone has already threatened them to stay away.

I realize why this location was chosen. I'm scared to death—I failed. Vincent failed. Everything we've been working for all along was a massive failure.

I need to get to the shore.

I duck behind a car near the edge of the parking lot. There's a lot of fighting between me and the shoreline. Before I can make my move, Beckett crouches down next to me.

"What's your plan?" he asks.

"I need to get as close to the shore as possible," I reply.

"Me too."

I stare through one of the car's windows, but all I see is chaos. I can't make anything out; I can't even decipher who are friends or foes.

"Together," Beckett says, taking my hand and squeezing it.

I squeeze back.

He drops my hand to grab his gun, and we take off into the fight.

There isn't much room for cover, so the only thing we can do is run and try not to draw attention to ourselves. When we do, we fire back.

Beckett stays by my side as we run. Despite everything we've been through, we trust each other on the battlefield. I cover the left side. He covers the right. Neither of us worries about the other failing at their job.

I see Lennox fighting with a man, so I shoot that man in the head. Lennox whips around, sees me, and smiles his gratitude.

I wish I could do more. I wish I could help ensure everyone I love and care about is safe. But right now, I have to be focused on only one person.

"Duck," I yell, pushing Beckett to the ground to narrowly avoid a bullet.

We both start firing back as soon as we hit the ground. A moment later, Beckett grabs the collar of my shirt, and then we're back on our feet and taking off.

I run as fast as I can, trying to keep up with Beckett running faster than before. It takes me a second, but I see his intended destination. A row of cars is parked a few yards away.

I pick up my speed, and we dive down between two cars.

"You hurt?" Beckett asks, inspecting me closely.

"No, I'm fine," I say, out of breath.

He nods. "Catch your breath before we move again."

I carefully peer through one of the car windows. Beckett does the same.

"We need to go left," I say.

"No, right," Beckett says.

Our eyes meet. I'm sure his family is to the right, but I have to go left.

"Stay safe," is all I say. Then I run out from behind the car toward her.

She's riding in one of Vincent's SUVs, but they've been completely ambushed. She'll be fine as long as she stays in the car; it's bulletproof and safe. Just stay in the car.

I run, shooting down men left and right as I get closer. It's my job to protect her.

Suddenly one of the SUV's doors opens.

"No, keep the door closed!" I shout.

But she doesn't listen.

The door opens, and she takes off.

Fuck.

I run faster.

"Who is she?" Beckett asks suddenly from beside me.

"Someone who needs our help," I respond.

He nods and picks up his speed.

I stop running to get a better aim and quickly shoot down three men chasing her. But she's still not safe.

Beckett keeps running after her.

I keep shooting.

My adrenaline is out of control as I resume sprinting, trying to keep a perimeter around her while Beckett catches up to her.

"I've got you. I'm here to protect you," Beckett's words reach my ears.

Thank god.

"Get her back into the SUV!" I shout.

Beckett carries her as she shakes in his arm, connecting her eyes with my own.

"Stay in the car. You're safe there. Trust me."

She nods.

We jog to the car. I lead the way and Beckett carries her behind me.

I don't see people—all I see are enemies. I shoot anyone that comes near us regardless of their alliance. Enemies or allies—it makes no difference to me right now. I just need her safe.

Beckett quickly helps her back into the bulletproof SUV and slams the door shut. The driver immediately takes off, now having a clear path out of the mayhem.

I need a car. I need to go after her. I need to make sure she's okay.

Odette knew about her. She knew—that's why she chose this location.

If my decision wasn't made before, it is now.

"Who was that?" Beckett asks, confused as hell.

"It doesn't matter."

He stares after the car, though.

"Ask me again," I say.

"Who was that?"

I shake my head. "No, not that. Ask me what you asked me on the drive here."

His eyes widen, and he holds his breath.

"Ask me," I whisper, pulling him behind a building so we can't be seen or interrupted.

"Who do you choose?" he asks, his voice cracking.

"I choose you."

27

BECKETT

RI CHOSE ME.

She chose me.

Nothing is official yet, and I have no idea what it means, but she chose me. She wants me, and that's all I need.

It's been a week since I last saw her. She snuck away in the middle of the battle soon after she told me. I went back into the battle, looking for my brother and his family. They're missing, but the fact that Odette continues the war reassures me that they are alive and safe somewhere.

I haven't talked to Odette in person either. The only people I've been with lately are Gage, Lennox, and Hayes.

We've been searching for Enzo and his family. Trying to get Ri to talk to us. Trying to find a way to end Odette without hurting Ri.

We all agreed that we have to let Ryker continue to help Odette. If she was honest with him, then she won't hurt Ri as long as he's helping her.

But keeping everyone I love safe is a challenge when every criminal organization and gang in the area has decided to fight on Odette's side. Between her and Ryker, they've rallied them all. They convinced them it's time to take down Corsi and that she has a way to take over everything he has. She told them Enzo, and his empire have always been allies with Corsi, so they need to be taken down as well.

I feel torn between my brother and those I've always considered family, and Ri, a woman I love with everything inside me, who I've always tried to protect.

For now, I don't have to choose, but there will come a time when I will. On the battlefield, in the moment, I chose Ri. I stayed by her side and protected her, but that was only because I didn't know exactly where my brother was. *But who would I choose if I actually had to decide?*

The four of us are currently in a hotel room, gathering any intel we can on the whereabouts of my brother and his family while trying to get in contact with Ri. But she hasn't reached out, and neither has Corsi to finish the game. Her declaration is getting less and less certain with every day that passes.

I'm staring at a computer screen, tapping into security systems, phone lines, anything we can to gain info. It's the same thing I've been doing every day when suddenly my phone next to me buzzes. Hayes ran out to get coffee, so I assume it's him forgetting one of our coffee orders again.

I open a text, and my heart seizes.

Meet me at the church on tenth street. Midnight. Wear a nice suit.

I stand up, knocking my chair to the ground. "Holy hell."

"What?" Gage and Lennox say at the same time.

"I think Ri just texted me. She wants to meet tonight."

I hold out the phone to them. They both stand from their spots at the table and walk over to get a better look.

"Are you sure it's her? It could be a trap," Gage says.

I sigh and reconsider the text. He's always the one to bring me back to reality.

Lennox frowns. "Can you ask her something only she knows?"

I consider a minute before texting back.

What was the last question I asked you?

Her response comes a second later.

Who do you choose?

"It's her."

Gage nods, accepting my test.

"What do you think she wants? Should we go with you?" Lennox asks.

"Yes, I want you all with me, but I'm not sure what she wants."

"What who wants?" Hayes asks as he pushes through the door, carrying three cups of coffee.

"Ri texted me." I hold out the phone to Hayes, and he sets the coffee down before taking my phone from me.

He grins widely at me.

"What?" I ask, confused.

"Dude. She invited you to a church and told you to wear a suit. She chose you. What do you think she wants?"

I shrug, completely confused.

"She wants you there to get married," Hayes says.

"What? You're reading too much into this. Even if that's true, I'm still legally married to Odette."

"No, you're not," Gage says, holding his laptop up to me. "Your marriage to Odette has been annulled, effective two days ago."

My eyes widen. "Holy shit."

My heart starts hammering uncontrollably.

Are my dreams finally coming true? Do I really get Ri the rest of my life? Once we marry, can we find a way to stop Odette with the power of the Corsi empire behind us?

The guys all stare at me with smirks on their faces. Hayes is right. I'm getting married tonight.

———

My palms are sweaty as I walk into the church with Lennox, Hayes, and Gage behind me, all in our best suits. Soft piano music is playing as we enter, but otherwise, the church seems empty.

I spent the day pacing, sweating, and rereading the text message a million times, trying to figure out if I misunderstood. I bought a simple ring—one I think Ri will like, just in case it's true.

I didn't know how else to spend my day other than waiting and hoping.

I don't draw my gun, but the other three do as we walk down the aisle of the church. Beautiful stain-glass windows, wooden pews, and a stone floor give the moment a traditional feel.

Slowly, we make our way toward the front as my hopes drop of this being my wedding. This was probably just a secluded place Ri wanted to meet so we wouldn't be spotted together.

As we reach the end of the aisle, right in front of the pulpit, I see a man walk toward me. Before I can ask him a question, the music changes, and the doors at the back of the church open. Ri is standing in a wedding dress and a full veil over her face. She begins walking down the aisle with Corsi escorting her.

Oh my god. This is really happening.

The guys smile at me as they put their guns away and stand behind me as if they're my groomsmen. We all turn and watch Ri walk down the aisle.

Her dress is one for a princess—full and puffy. I'm sure she wore it to tease us for always calling her a princess, not because it fits her style. I can barely see beneath her veil, but her long, raven hair sticks out around the edges.

I don't think I breathe as she slowly walks down the aisle with her father. He looks at me stone-faced, emotionless. I have no idea what he thinks of all of this, but I'm thankful he's honoring Ri's wishes.

I won.

I get to spend the rest of my life with her.

I stare at her stomach. She said to win, you either had to get her pregnant or accomplish some other secret method of winning.

Did I win because I was the one who impregnated her? If so, it had to have been from before.

Or did I win because I won her heart?

I can't wait to ask her that and a million other questions soon. She's mine, and together we will conquer the world.

They reach the end of the aisle, and I hold out my arm for her to take it.

Corsi looks at me. "Protect Rialta with your life."

"I swear I will," I vow.

He nods and then passes Ri's hand from his arm to mine. Together, she and I take two steps toward the minister.

"Can I lift your veil? I want to look you in the eyes when I marry you," I ask her.

She nods.

Slowly, I lift her veil, careful not to mess up her hair or makeup. I'm expecting to see Ri's beautiful big eyes staring back at me with a teasing gaze, but that's not what I get. In fact, Ri isn't the one staring back at me at all—it's the woman I helped Ri save.

I blink in disbelief. This has to be a mistake.

"Who are you?" I ask.

"Rialta Corsi," she replies.

———

Thank you for reading Tortured Hero! I hope you enjoyed it! Beckett and Ri's story concludes in Dangerous Princess

ALSO BY ELLA MILES

LIES SERIES:

Lies We Share: A Prologue

Vicious Lies

Desperate Lies

Fated Lies

Cruel Lies

Dangerous Lies

Endless Lies

SINFUL TRUTHS:

Sinful Truth #1

Twisted Vow #2

Reckless Fall #3

Tangled Promise #4

Fallen Love #5

Broken Anchor #6

TRUTH OR LIES:

Taken by Lies #1

Betrayed by Truths #2

Trapped by Lies #3

Stolen by Truths #4

Possessed by Lies #5

Consumed by Truths #6

DIRTY SERIES:

Dirty Obsession

Dirty Addiction

Dirty Revenge

Dirty: The Complete Series

ALIGNED SERIES:

Aligned: Volume 1 (Free Series Starter)

Aligned: Volume 2

Aligned: Volume 3

Aligned: Volume 4

Aligned: The Complete Series Boxset

UNFORGIVABLE SERIES:

Heart of a Thief

Heart of a Liar

Heart of a Prick

Unforgivable: The Complete Series Boxset

MAYBE, DEFINITELY SERIES:

Maybe Yes

Maybe Never

Maybe Always

Definitely Yes

Definitely No

Definitely Forever

STANDALONES:

Pretend I'm Yours

Pretend We're Over

Finding Perfect

Savage Love

Too Much

Not Sorry

Hate Me or Love Me: An Enemies to Lovers Romance Collection

ABOUT THE AUTHOR

Ella Miles writes steamy romance, including everything from dark suspense romance that will leave you on the edge of your seat to contemporary romance that will leave you laughing out loud or crying. Most importantly, she wants you to feel everything her characters feel as you read.

Ella is currently living her own happily ever after near the Rocky Mountains with her high school sweetheart husband. Her heart is also taken by her goofy five year old black lab who is scared of everything, including her own shadow.

Ella is a USA Today Bestselling Author & Top 50 Bestselling Author.

Stalk Ella at:
www.ellamiles.com
ella@ellamiles.com